A DUEL OF JEWELS

Katerina's French stepmother tries to make her agree to marry a very rich but elderly Duke because they have very little money. She refuses.

Frustrated and angry her stepmother pushes her out through the front door and Katerina finds herself alone on the pavement.

Next door Prince Michel of Saronia is furious because Lady Lettice Ling, with whom he is having an *affaire de coeur*, has refused to wear the crown jewels of his country. She says she is superstitious about emeralds, they quarrel and the Prince storms out of the house.

Outside he discovers Katerina whom he befriends.

He has made a wager with the Prince Fredrich of Heinburg that his crown jewels are the more superior and he is determined to win it.

He persuades Katerina to wear the jewels during the competition and because she looks so beautiful in them he wins the wager.

Then Prince Fredrich tries to seduce Katerina and the two men have a fierce argument.

How Katerina saves Prince Michel's life and how he finds an answer to her own problems is all told in s romantic story, the 493rd by Barbara Cartland.

A DUEL OF JEWELS

by

Barbara Cartland

SEVERN HOUSE PUBLISHERS

This first world edition published in Great Britain 1993 by
SEVERN HOUSE PUBLISHERS LTD of
9–15 High Street, Sutton, Surrey SM1 1DF.
First published in the USA 1993 by
SEVERN HOUSE PUBLISHERS INC of
475 Fifth Avenue, New York, NY 10017.

British Library·Cataloguing in Publication Data
Cartland, Barbara, 1902–
   A Duel of Jewels
   I. Title
   823.912 [F]

   ISBN 0-7278-4474-1

Typeset by Hewer Text Composition Services, Edinburgh.
Printed and bound in Great Britain by
Redwood Books, Trowbridge, Wiltshire.

AUTHOR'S NOTE

When recently I was writing a book called *Royal Jewels*, I was fascinated to find that the first crown jewels go back a long way in history.

In fact one of the first Orbs dates from the time of the Holy Roman Empire.

The most famous crown was that of the Emperor Charlemagne, whose tomb was opened by King Otto III in the year 1000.

The great Emperor was found perfectly preserved, sitting on his marble throne wearing his royal jewels, his white beard spread across his chest.

Perhaps the most romantic royal jewel was the earring which belonged to Queen Cleopatra, who gave it to her lover Mark Anthony as an aphrodisiac.

It was the most expensive drink that anybody has ever had because in those days pearls were the most valuable currency in the world. In fact one Roman Emperor ran his whole campaign on one of his mother-in-law's earrings.

The matching earring to the one Cleopatra dissolved was recently owned by the Duke of Abercorn.

He, however, sold it to Richard Burton who gave it to his beautiful film-star wife Elizabeth Taylor.

ABOUT THE AUTHOR

Barbara Cartland, the world's most famous romantic novelist, who is also an historian, playwright, lecturer, political speaker and television personality, has now written over 490 books and sold over 500 million copies all over the world.

She has also had many historical works published and has written four autobiographies as well as the biographies of her mother and that of her brother, Ronald Cartland, who was the first Member of Parliament to be killed in the last war. This book has a preface by Sir Winston Churchill and has just been republished with an introduction by the late Sir Arthur Bryant.

Love at the Helm, a novel written with the help and inspiration of the late Earl Mountbatten of Burma, great uncle of His Royal Highness The Prince of Wales, is being sold for the Mountbatten Memorial Trust.

She has broken the world record for the last thirteen years by writing an average of twenty-three books a year. In the *Guinness Book of Records* she is listed as the world's top-selling author.

Miss Cartland in 1978 sang an *Album of Love Songs* with the Royal Philharmonic Orchestra.

In private life Barbara Cartland, who is a Dame of Grace of the Order of St John of Jerusalem, Chairman of the St John Council in Hertfordshire and Deputy President of the St John Ambulance Brigade, has fought for better conditions and salaries for midwives and nurses.

She championed the cause for the elderly, in 1956 invoking a Government Enquiry into the "Housing Conditions of Old People".

In 1962 she had the law of England changed so that local authorities had to provide camps for their own gypsies. This has meant that since then thousands and thousands of gypsy children have been able to go to school which they had never been able to do in the past, as their caravans were moved every twenty-four hours by the police.

There are now fourteen camps in Hertfordshire and Barbara Cartland has her own Romany gypsy camp, called Barbaraville by the gypsies.

Her designs, "Decorating with Love", are being sold all over the U.S.A., and the National Home Fashions League made her, in 1981, "Woman of Achievement".

Barbara Cartland's book *Getting Older, Growing Younger* has been published in Great Britain and the U.S.A. and her fifth cookery book, *The Romance of Food*, is now being used by the House of Commons.

In 1984 she received, at Kennedy Airport, America's Bishop Wright Air Industry Award for her contribution to the development of aviation. In 1931 she and two R.A.F. officers thought of, and carried, the first aeroplane-towed glider air-mail.

During the war she was Chief Lady Welfare Officer in Bedfordshire looking after 20,000 service men and women. She thought of having a pool of wedding dresses at the War Office so a service bride could hire a gown for the day.

She bought 1,000 second-hand gowns without coupons for the A.T.S., the W.A.A.F.s and the W.R.E.N.S. In 1945 Barbara Cartland received the Certificate of Merit from Eastern Command.

In 1964 Barbara Cartland founded the National Association for Health of which she is the President, as a front for all the Health Stores and for any product made as alternative medicine.

This has now a £500,000,000 turnover a year, with one third going in export.

In January 1988 she received "La Medaille de Vermeil de la Ville de Paris" (the Gold Medal of Paris). This is the highest award to be given by the City of Paris for ACHIEVEMENT – 25 million books sold in France.

In March 1988 Barbara Cartland was asked by the Indian Government to open their Health Resort outside Delhi. This is almost the largest Health Resort in the world.

Barbara Cartland was received with great enthusiasm by her fans, who also fêted her at a reception in the city, and she received the gift of an embossed plate from the Government.

OTHER BOOKS BY
BARBARA CARTLAND

Romantic novels, over 490, the most recently published being:

Autobiographical and Biographical:

Historical:

Bewitching Women
The Outrageous Queen (The Story of Queen Christina
of Sweden)
The Scandalous Life of King Carol
The Private Life of Charles II
The Private Life of Elizabeth, Empress of Austria
Josephine, Empress of France
Diane de Poitiers
Metternich – The Passionate Diplomat
A Year of Royal Days
Royal Jewels
Royal Eccentrics
Royal Lovers

Sociology:

You in the Home	Etiquette
The Fascinating Forties	The Many Facets of Love
Marriage for Moderns	Sex and the Teenager
Be Vivid, Be Vital	The Book of Charm
Love, Life and Sex	Living Together
Vitamins for Vitality	The Youth Secret
Husbands and Wives	The Magic of Honey
Men are Wonderful	The Book of Beauty and
	Health

Keep Young and Beautiful by Barbara Cartland and
    Elinor Glyn
Etiquette for Love and Romance
Barbara Cartland's Book of Health

Cookery:

Barbara Cartland's Health Food Cookery Book
Food for Love
Magic of Honey Cookbook
Recipes for Lovers
The Romance of Food

Editor of:

The Common Problem by Ronald Cartland (with a preface by the Rt. Hon. the Earl of Selborne, P.C.)
Barbara Cartland's Library of Love
Library of Ancient Wisdom
Written with Love. Passionate love letters selected by Barbara Cartland

Drama:

Blood Money
French Dressing

Philosophy:

Touch the Stars

Radio Operetta:

The Rose and the Violet (Music by Mark Lubbock) Performed in 1942.

Radio Plays:

The Caged Bird: An episode in the life of Elizabeth Empress of Austria. Performed in 1957.

General:

Barbara Cartland's Book of Useless Information with
a Foreword by the Earl Mountbatten of Burma.
(In aid of the United World Colleges)
Love and Lovers (Picture Book)
The Light of Love (Prayer Book)
Barbara Cartland's Scrapbook
(In aid of the Royal Photographic Museum)
Romantic Royal Marriages
Barbara Cartland's Book of Celebrities
Getting Older, Growing Younger

Verse:

Lines on Life and Love

Music:

An Album of Love Songs sung with the Royal Philharmonic Orchestra.

Films:

The Flame is Love
A Hazard of Hearts
The Lady and the Highwayman

Cartoons:

Barbara Cartland Romances (Book of Cartoons) has
recently been published in the U.S.A., Great Britain,
and other parts of the world.

Children:

A Children's Pop-Up Book: Princess to the Rescue

Videos:

A Hazard of Hearts
The Lady and The Highwayman

Chapter One

1890

"I will not marry him!" Katerina said firmly.

Her stepmother gave a scream of protest. "Do not be so ridiculous," she snapped. "You know as well as I do that your father has left us very little money and the Duc is rich. His family is one of the oldest in the whole of France." Lady Colwin was talking very quickly as the French always do and with a distinctive accent.

She was an attractive woman whom Lord Colwin had married after he had been a widower for a year and found it intolerable to be alone. His only child, Katerina, was at school in England. As Ambassador to France he found the large house and the constant entertaining he had to do abroad impossible without a wife beside him.

Before he quite realised his plight, Madame Desirée

Beauvais had realised it very clearly. With the expertise and charm for which the French are traditionally famous, she made herself indispensable to him.

Katerina was horrified when she learned, while she was still at school, that her father had re-married.

She had adored her beautiful mother, who had been the daughter of the Earl of Edgemont. Lady Esther had never been strong, and after Katerina was born she was unable to have any more children.

She, however, followed her husband round the world to his various posts.

He was noted as being one of the most brilliant diplomats England had ever produced.

His wife went with him from Paris to Vienna, from Vienna to Madrid, from Madrid to Paris. It was perhaps the entertaining and the fact that she was always "on show" almost every hour of her waking life that killed her. She could not stand the pace and grew thinner and thinner. Yet she forced herself to be vivacious and charming, while she was actually fading away.

When she died Lord Colwin felt as if his world had come to an end. However he was too much of a professional to let that actually happen. He carried on alone until Desirée Beauvais showed him very clearly that she could make things more comfortable and much more pleasant if she was his wife.

They were married, and although Lord Colwin was more or less happy at the arrangement, he died within the year.

To his second wife it was a disaster she had not expected.

To his daughter it was a tragedy.

Katerina had been in Paris for only a month when her father fell ill, and she hardly left his bedside. He died in the British Embassy and the funeral took place in the Embassy church.

Lord Colwin had been extremely popular with the French as he was in every other country where he had served. So many wished to attend the funeral service that it would have been impossible to find room for them all in the small church.

A memorial service was therefore held at a later date when everybody told Katerina how much they would miss her father.

At the same time the Frenchmen looked at her admiringly and paid her compliments which made her blush.

She was indisputably very lovely. She was like her mother, but with an indefinable difference which was extremely striking. She was more than just beautiful, for there was something unmistakably spiritual about her.

She made every man think she was an angel. Or perhaps one of the goddesses come down from Olympus.

Because she was in deep mourning, she could not go to parties or receptions such as she had expected to enjoy with her father.

The same of course applied also to her stepmother. However Lady Colwin managed to have what she thought of as "discreet At Homes" for some of her more intimate friends. They developed into occasions that were certainly not in keeping with her mourning gowns.

Yet it was at a luncheon which Katerina attended to make the numbers even that the Duc de Soisson first saw her.

He was a man of forty-five and had already had two wives and a number of children. Yet he knew the moment he saw Katerina that he wanted her.

Almost before she realised who he was he had approached her stepmother.

To Katerina the idea of being married so soon after her father's death was unthinkable. Worse still would be to be married to a man so much older than she was!

She had heard also that the Duc had an unpleasant reputation. When his hand touched hers she felt as if she had come into contact with a serpent.

"I hate him!" she said now. "How can I possibly marry a man who makes me shiver every time he comes near me?"

"*Mon Dieu*, but you are so stupid! I cannot believe what I am hearing!" her stepmother protested. "Any girl with an atom of sense would be overjoyed and thrilled at the idea of becoming a Duchesse." Katerina did not answer so she went on: "I have seen the Duc's château near Lyon, which is magnificent, and besides that he has a house in the Champs Elysées which is filled with treasures which somehow managed to escape destruction in the Revolution."

"I would not be marrying his treasures," Katerina objected, "but the Duc!"

Her stepmother flung up her hands in a theatrical gesture. "How can I get it into your foolish head," she asked, "that marriage is not just a question of making love? It is security, it is protection. In this case, it is knowing that you will be one of the most important hostesses in the whole of France. Could any girl ask for more?"

"I want a great deal more," Katerina replied.

She thought as she spoke that her stepmother's behaviour was not only over-dramatic, but also very un-English. She could not therefore discuss the matter quietly as she would have done with her father. Her stepmother was screaming and throwing her arms about. She gabbled so quickly that Katerina was not sure whether she was speaking in French or English.

Lady Colwin walked across the room and back again before she said, "We are practically penniless – do you hear? Admittedly your father had a large salary, but it died with him and the money he invested during his lifetime is very little. What there is would hardly keep us in shoelaces, let alone anything else!"

Katerina knew this way of talking was exaggerated. At the same time, she was aware that her father had spent his money generously.

She had always known the Colwin family had very little money. Before he was made a peer, her father had been Sir William Colwin, the 5th Baronet. The name went back to the twelfth century.

That, however, did not mean that the Colwins had a large bank balance. She was aware that it was only her father's brilliant brain which had made him rise in the diplomatic service. He had finally crowned his career in the most important position of all as Ambassador to France.

Katerina remembered that her mother had always been careful with what money they did have. But Madame Desirée had purchased clothes, furs and jewels as if she was married to a millionaire.

After her father's funeral she and her stepmother had been obliged to leave the Embassy immediately so that the new Ambassador could move in.

Lady Colwin rented a house in the Rue St Cloud, just off the Champs Elysées. It was expensive because it had large reception rooms where she could entertain her friends.

Katerina knew that she considered now that the expense had been worth while because the Duc de Soisson had proposed.

Lady Colwin was wildly elated when he did so. So she found it almost impossible to believe that her stepdaughter would refuse such an offer. She had the opportunity not only of being rich, but also of having an unassailable position in the social world. Lady Colwin had been so certain there would be no question of Katerina refusing such a catch that she had embraced the Duc fondly.

"You must be married quietly," she said, "because we are still in mourning for poor, dear William. I can make the excuse that if you do not marry Katerina at once, she will return to London to live with her father's relatives."

"I will marry her tomorrow, Madame, if you will allow me to do so," the Duc replied.

Lady Colwin had laughed. "That is just how I thought you would feel," she said coquettishly. "You have always, *mon cher*, had the reputation of being an ardent lover."

The Duc was pleased at the compliment and she went on: "Katerina is a very lucky girl. I know that she will make you happy and of course give you the son for whom you have longed."

She saw the Duc stiffen as if he resented her speaking about it. It was a very sore point that neither of his wives had given him a son. Instead he had four daughters. This made the heir presumptive to the title an elderly cousin who had remained unmarried.

Thrilled and delighted by what she heard, Lady Colwin arranged with the Duc that he should come to luncheon the next day. Then she would leave him alone with Katerina when the meal was finished.

Quite unsuspecting, Katerina was told in the morning to put on one of her prettiest gowns. When she asked why, she was told that her stepmother had a visitor.

When she learnt it was the Duc, she wondered if in fact he was one of her stepmother's *chers amis*.

She had been very innocent when she first came to Paris. She had no idea that her stepmother had had a somewhat chequered career before she married her father. But the servants talked and the conversation of their guests contained unmistakable innuendos. She would therefore have been very stupid if she had not become aware within a week of her arrival that her stepmother was somewhat notorious in Paris.

At first Katerina was extremely shocked. She had never imagined a woman who was not pure and very respectable would take her mother's place.

Then she told herself it was not for her to criticise. But she began to wonder how she could return to England and what she would do once she got there.

Because Lord Colwin had worked abroad for so many years, he had given up the house he had first occupied with his wife in Buckinghamshire. It seemed a sensible thing to do. If he was in Russia, Vienna or anywhere else, he could hardly keep coming backwards and forwards. It was in any case a luxury he could not afford.

In the long summer holidays Katerina always joined her father and mother wherever they might be. But at Easter and Christmas she stayed with her relations. One of these had recently died and the other was very old. She therefore could not think to whom she could go.

Her grandfather, the Earl of Edgemont, was dead. His eldest son who had inherited the title was Governor of one of the provinces of India.

At luncheon the Duc and her stepmother chatted away at a tremendous speed in French all the way through the meal.

Katerina did not listen closely to the conversation. She was wondering how she could return to England and to whom she could write about it.

She was therefore surprised when her stepmother said: "I want you, Katerina, to take *Monsieur le Duc* into the drawing room. I have something I have to do before I can join you."

Katerina followed her stepmother out of the dining room and went into the drawing room.

It was the largest room in the house. It was well furnished, with some quite pleasant pictures on the walls. There was also masses of flowers, which Katerina thought was a quite unnecessary extravagance.

She wondered why her stepmother had bought so many. They were not, as far as she knew, entertaining this afternoon or tomorrow.

The Duc shut the door and walked towards her.

He stood for a moment looking down at her and thinking how lovely she was. In fact she was more exquisitely beautiful than any English woman he could remember having seen before.

"*Ma petite*," he said softly, "you must know why I am here."

Katerina opened her eyes wider. "I supposed . . you had . . come to . . see stepmama," she replied.

It flashed through her mind that perhaps he was going to tell her that he wanted to marry her stepmother. If he did so, she thought, it would be extremely fortunate and the best thing that could happen. It would mean that her stepmother would have plenty of money and a position which she wanted. She herself could then go back to England and perhaps find something to do.

"I am here," the Duc was saying, "because, as I told your stepmother last night, I want you to be my wife."

Katerina stared at him and thought she could not have heard aright. "Your . . wife?" she stammered.

"*Oui,*" the Duc said. "I think we shall be very happy together, and I have a great deal to teach you about love."

The way he spoke and the look in his eyes made Katerina take several steps away from him. Almost instinctively her hands went up as if to protect herself.

"No," she exclaimed, "no! You cannot mean it!"

"I do mean it," the Duc insisted, "and your step-mother, who is of course your guardian, has given her permission. We will be married at once and we will go to my château until you are out of mourning. Then, my beautiful one, we will enjoy ourselves in Paris."

"No! No!" Katerina cried again, "I cannot . . marry you . . I do . . not . . love . . you." She stammered over the words and the Duc laughed.

"So young – so innocent!" he said as if he was speaking to himself. "I will teach you about love, *ma petite*, and it will be one of the most exciting things I have ever done." He made a move towards her.

When he would have taken her in his arms she managed deftly to avoid them. Frantically she ran towards the door.

"No, no, no!" she exclaimed breathlessly as she

reached it, "I am .. sorry .. but I cannot .. marry .. you!"

She was gone before he could prevent her from leaving him.

At the same time he was unperturbed. He was well aware of his value in the social field. He had understood Lady Colwin's excitement at the idea of his marrying Katerina.

"She is very young and very shy," he told himself.

There was a touch of fire in his eyes as he thought of how he could change her once she belonged to him.

It was long after he had left before Lady Colwin learned from Katerina that she had actually refused the Duc's proposal. She was not aware of it at first because Katerina had gone to her room and locked herself in.

"How can I marry an old man like that?" she asked herself. Even the idea of it was horrifying.

She had dreamt of love – of course she had. Her father and mother had always been blissfully happy together. She had believed that one day she would find a man as handsome and as clever as her father. They would be drawn instinctively to each other because they would think the same and feel the same.

Her dream man would be only a little older than herself. It would not matter whether he was rich or poor if God had made them for each other. That would ensure their happiness for ever.

She came downstairs for dinner, hoping that the Duc had not been invited to that meal.

Her stepmother had rushed towards her the moment

she entered the drawing room. She kissed her affectionately.

"This is wonderful news, *ma chère*!" she exclaimed. "Now there will be no more financial problems, you shall have the most splendid trousseau any girl has ever possessed."

Katerina disentangled herself from her stepmother's embrace. "If you are talking about my marriage to the Duc," she said, "I have refused him."

"You have – refused him?" Lady Colwin screamed. It was a sound that seemed to echo round the room.

"Of course," Katerina replied. "He is old and I positively dislike him!"

It was then the row started and continued for nearly an hour.

Finally, Lady Colwin completely lost her temper. "I am your guardian," she said, "and you will marry the Duc if I have to drag you unconscious to the altar! I will not allow you to make a fool of yourself – or me. You will be his wife, and you should thank God on your knees."

As she finished shrieking out the words, the door opened and a manservant said: "*Le dîner est servi, Madame.*"

Because she was upset and embarrassed by her stepmother's behaviour, Katerina walked immediately to the door and Lady Colwin followed her.

"You will marry him!" she said in English so that the servants would not understand. "And to make sure you do so, I will keep you locked in your bedroom without food until you write and tell the Duc that you would be honoured to be his wife."

Katerina had reached the hall. As the servant went on towards the dining room she turned to face her stepmother. "I am sorry, *belle-mere*," she said quietly, "but I have to make you understand that I would not marry the Duc if he was the last man on earth. I would starve to death rather than be his wife."

Lady Colwin gave a shrill cry that said better than words that she had completely lost her self-control. "Very well," she said, "if you want to starve you shall starve!"

She struck Katerina violently on her shoulder. Then she pulled her towards the front door, opened it and pushed her outside.

"Stay out there until you learn on which side your bread is buttered!" she shouted. Her voice ended on a high note.

She slammed the door shut and Katerina heard her bolt it.

It was now nearly 9 o'clock, for her stepmother liked to dine late, and the sun had sunk. Dusk was just creeping up the sky.

Katerina stood on the pavement wondering what she should do and where she could go.

Because it was not very long since her father's death, the British Embassy was the only other house she was familiar with. But she felt she could not return there at this time of the night and ask the new Ambassador to take her in. She had only shaken him by the hand, and really did not know him at all.

She wondered how long it would be before her stepmother relented and opened the door.

In the meantime it was extremely embarrassing to be standing on the pavement in what had been a very expensive evening-gown.

She did not even have a wrap to cover her bare shoulders. She had expected to be dining alone with her stepmother. She was therefore not wearing one of the black gowns they had bought immediately after her father's death.

Instead she had put on one that was white.

It had been extremely expensive because it had been bought in Paris.

Her father had always disliked black, especially mourning. "It is far too often just hypocrisy," he would say.

When Katerina arrived Lady Colwin had sneered at her very English clothes. In her usual impulsive manner Lady Colwin had carried Katerina off to the most expensive shops in the Rue de la Paix. She had fitted her stepdaughter out with a number of charming gowns designed by the most famous couturiers in Paris. When her father had died a fortnight later, it became just another large bill to add to the numerous others run up by Lady Colwin.

"What shall . . I do? What shall I . . do?" Katerina asked herself.

Then, when a man who passed looked at her in a strange way, she was frightened.

She put her hands up to her face. "Help me . . papa . . please . . help me," she begged. "I know you would not . . allow me to be in this . . predicament if you were . . alive, so wherever . . you are at this moment . . you must . . help me . . I do not know . . what to . . do."

She shut her eyes and her hands covered them.

Then she heard a voice ask: "Is anything wrong? May I help you?"

"I do not believe that you are really refusing to do as I ask you!" Prince Michel said sharply.

"It is a ridiculous idea and I utterly refuse!" Lady Lettice replied.

She was looking very lovely as she lay back on the sofa, a cushion behind her head and her elegant feet raised as if she was exhausted. She was exceedingly beautiful, as she well knew.

The acclamation she had received in London and later in Paris had made her very certain there was no need for her ever to do anything she did not want to do.

"I cannot believe you are refusing to appear after you promised me," the Prince said, "and after I agreed the bet with Prince Fredrich that you would wear my jewels."

"That is what you arranged," Lady Lettice said petulantly, "but you omitted to tell me that the crown jewels consisted mostly of emeralds. I do not like emeralds. They are unlucky for me, and they do not become me."

The Prince made an impatient sound as he walked across the room to lean against the mantelpiece.

"I admit it was a rather idiotic idea," he said slowly, "but Prince Fredrich annoyed me by bumptiously boasting how fine his crown jewels are, when I am quite certain mine are superior."

"Does it really matter, one way or the other?" Lady Lettice asked in a bored voice.

"It matters to me as you well know," the Prince replied. "There is a stake of ten thousand francs, and I have no wish to have Fredrich shouting all over Paris that he has won such a sum from me, and that the Heinburg jewels are superior to those of Saronia."

Lady Lettice's lips parted, but she did not speak. She found it extremely tedious that two men should fight over anything that was not herself.

She would have appreciated a duel in which the two Princes were fighting for her favours. But to be betting as to whose crown jewels were the best was, in her opinion, such a waste of time that she had no wish to be involved.

The Prince, however, had different ideas. "You promised me, Lettice!" he protested. "You know you promised and I trusted you. Because you are so beautiful, I know the judges will all look at you and award me the prize, regardless of whether my jewels are better or not."

He was speaking in a more persuasive manner now simply because he wished to have his own way.

But Lady Lettice was adamant, and she merely shrugged her shoulders. "I do not like emeralds!" she said in the way a child might have spoken.

"Oh, for God's sake!" the Prince exclaimed. "Try

to be sensible about this. If you refuse to come to the party you will let me down, and anyway you know that I want you with me."

"If you want me as much as that," Lady Lettice said, "we can go to the Café Anglais and be together. After all, everyone will be there, and it will be far more amusing than a stuffy dinner with Prince Fredrich, whom I have always thought a bore!"

"So have I," the Prince agreed. "But we made a wager and I cannot go back on my word."

"Why do you not just give him the ten thousand francs and forget it?" Lady Lettice said.

"I'll be damned if I do!" Prince Michel declared.

He walked across the room and back again, thinking as he did so how tiresome Lady Lettice was being.

Admittedly she was outstandingly beautiful. He had been attracted to her the minute he had seen her in London at Buckingham Palace.

As the daughter of a Marquess, despite her reputation, which apparently had escaped the ears of Queen Victoria, she was still present on State occasions both at Windsor Castle and at Buckingham Palace. But Lady Lettice had always been spoilt and determined to get her own way.

Her father had refused his permission when she wanted to marry the penniless younger son of an unimportant Peer. She had therefore run away with David Larson on her eighteenth birthday. They had been married in defiance of her father's wishes.

When he was drowned the following year in a

boating accident, the Marquess had been delighted. He set about trying to find for his daughter the sort of husband of whom he approved.

Lady Lettice, however, announced that she had had enough of marriage. She had taken lover after lover, and the gossips shook their heads and never stopped whispering about her.

More and more acclaimed, she was undoubtedly the most beautiful woman in England. When Prince Michel of Saronia saw her at Buckingham Palace he had been as instantly bowled over by her, as many other men had been before him.

Because he in his turn was very handsome and had an irresistible charm, he had swept her off her feet.

When he left England he had taken her with him to Paris.

In France Lady Lettice had enjoyed the same success as in England. The French, however, expressed themselves more dramatically and more extravagantly.

She was delighted when she knew she had the whole of Paris talking about her. Almost every man was ready to lay his heart at her feet.

She was now being difficult just because Prince Michel was so persistent. What was more, he was showing an interest in something that did not concern herself.

She was well aware that Prince Fredrich of Heinburg was a tiresome, boastful man. Of Prussian blood, he was always wanting to get the better of his contemporaries in some way or another. He was jealous of Prince Michel, and he had forced the wager simply because he wished to assert himself.

Once it was made, Prince Michel had taken it seriously and sent an aide-de-camp to Saronia for the crown jewels.

When they were brought to him, he realised that it would be improbable that the Heinburg collection could in any way equal his own. They had been handed down with additions over five centuries.

The Saronian principality was a small but prosperous country with fertile land. Some of the finest horses in Europe, second only to those of Hungary, were bred there.

Heinburg was also small, but it was a dull principality with nothing particularly to recommend it.

The Prince made one more effort. "Be a sport, Lettice," he begged, "and stop being difficult. If you will wear these jewels tonight, I will buy you anything you fancy in the Rue de la Paix tomorrow."

"I am not wearing emeralds!" Lady Lettice said positively and her lips closed in a tight line.

"Very well, if that is your attitude, I will go without you," the Prince said. "I hope you can find someone to take you to dinner because I am leaving now."

He picked up the case containing the jewels and walking out of the room slammed the door behind him.

Lady Lettice heard his footsteps hurrying down the stairs. She thought perhaps she was making a mistake to let him go.

"Michel! Michel!" she called, sitting up on the sofa.

But it was too late. The servants on duty at the front door had already opened the door for the Prince and he saw his carriage was waiting.

He handed the jewel-case to the footman who was holding open the door.

As he did so he saw to his surprise an extremely lovely woman in an evening-gown, but without a wrap, standing on the pavement. She was holding her hands up to her face. He thought perhaps she had been in an accident and had been injured.

He walked towards her.

Chapter Two

"Are you all right?" the Prince asked in French.

For a moment Katerina did not move. Then slowly she took her hands away from her eyes.

She looked up at the Prince and he thought he had never in his life seen anyone so beautiful. There were tears on her cheeks and her huge eyes were swimming with them. At the same time, her skin had the translucence of a pearl. She had a little straight nose, and her lips which trembled a little were very moving.

"I . . am . . all right," she said in a voice which was hardly audible.

The Prince looked around him.

"You are here alone?" he asked. "Where are your attendants?"

"I am . . alone," Katerina stammered.

The Prince was astonished, feeling it impossible that

anyone should look so lovely and not be protected by an escort.

"Perhaps you are lost?" he suggested.

Katerina snatched at the suggestion. "Y . . yes," she agreed, "I am . . lost."

"Let me drive you to wherever you are staying," Prince Michel suggested. "My carriage, as you see, awaits."

He indicated it with his hand. But Katerina hesitated. Then she told herself that if she was allowed back into the house, her stepmother might hit her again.

She would also insist, as she had before, that she must marry the Duc. Although it seemed strange, this was an opportunity for escape. She had never imagined it could come in such a manner.

Taking her hesitation as an affirmative, the Prince said: "Let me help you into my carriage. Then we can decide where it is you want to go."

Katerina thought that if she remained outside the front door any longer, her stepmother might pull her back into the house. She felt she could not bear to hear the arguments all over again. Her shoulder was aching from the blow her stepmother had struck her. Without speaking, she stepped into the carriage and the Prince joined her.

As he did so he said to the footman: "Tell the coachman to drive round the Place de la Concorde until I tell him where I want to go."

"*Oui, Monsieur*," the footman said. He climbed up on the box and the horses started off.

The Prince turned sideways to look at Katerina who was wiping her eyes. He knew he had not been mistaken in thinking she was the loveliest woman he had ever seen. He was also aware that she was expensively gowned. There was a small string of perfect pearls at her throat.

"Now, tell me what has happened to you," he asked in a coaxing tone which no woman had ever been able to resist. "I think in fact you have run away."

Katerina just nodded her head. At the same time, she told herself that no one must ever know that her stepmother had thrown her out of the house. She could imagine how the gossips would chatter. How could she allow them to know that her father's daughter had been pushed out into the street?

"If you have run away," the Prince continued, "there must be a good reason for it, and I would like you to trust me." He paused for a moment before he said: "I have always considered myself to be rather good at solving problems, so tell me about yourself."

"I . . I cannot do . . that."

The Prince sighed. "I am disappointed, but if you will not confide in me, will you at least tell me where you wish to go?"

Katerina clasped her hands together and he was aware that she was trembling. She was of course terrified of the future and of her stepmother. She hated the Duc! She hated him so violently that she knew if he should approach her she would want to scream.

Perhaps, she thought, if she told him she really felt like that, he would no longer want her. Then her common sense told her that was unlikely. If the Duc was determined to marry her, he would not take "No" for an answer. Once she was his wife, there would be no escape. She realised that the Prince was waiting for her to speak. She turned to look at him, her eyes very revealing as she stammered:

"I .. I cannot .. go back .. so I have .. nowhere to g .. go."

The Prince stared at her. The last rays of the sun which was sinking low in the sky came through the carriage window. They turned her fair hair into a halo of light.

"How can it be possible," he asked, "that looking as lovely as you do you should be in such a predicament?"

Katerina looked shyly away from him before she said as if she was speaking to herself: "I .. c .. cannot go back .. I .. cannot!"

The Prince suddenly remembered that on the seat opposite them the footman had placed the big box containing the crown jewels. It was then he knew that Fate had been unexpectedly kind to him. "I think," he said slowly, "you need time to think over what has happened, whatever it may be. While you are doing so, I have a suggestion to make." He knew that Katerina was listening, although she did not reply, and he went on: "I am Prince Michel of Saronia. I have made a silly wager with Prince Fredrich of Heinburg that my crown jewels are better than his. He has arranged that at a party tonight we are each to bring a beautiful woman who will show off our respective jewels."

Because it sounded such a strange story, Katerina turned her head to look at him wide-eyed.

"The lady who was to wear my jewels," the Prince explained, "has refused to do so at the very last minute. Now I am thinking that perhaps my luck has not failed me after all." He smiled before he went on. "Or else the gods have sent me a substitute in what seems to me to be a remarkable and somewhat wonderful manner." His voice was very compelling.

As he finished speaking, Katerina asked in a whisper: "D .. do you mean .. me?"

"Of course I mean you," the Prince replied, "if you will be so kind and generous as to help me out of a very embarrassing situation. Otherwise I am certain Prince Fredrich will make the most of it and I shall be ignominiously defeated, even before the competition has begun."

Katerina stared at him and he pleaded: "Please, beautiful lady, please, help me."

She hesitated for a moment, then asked herself, Why not? "Suppose," she said in a very small voice, "that your .. jewels do not look .. right on .. me?"

"I think that you will make them look so beautiful that everyone watching will be blinded by them," the Prince said positively. "Need I tell you that Prince Fredrich is a German, and a very bumptious man who needs taking down a peg or two."

Katerina gave a little laugh as if she could not help it and the Prince said: "I know you are going to say yes, and I can never thank you enough – thank you, thank you! Although I do not believe you are real!"

Katerina laughed again and he asked: "What is your name?"

"Katerina," she said without thinking. Even as she spoke she told herself it would be a very great mistake for him to know who she actually was. People would be shocked and horrified to learn that the daughter of the late Lord Colwin was alone on the street at night. Actually at the mercy of any man who might stop and speak to her.

"That is a Russian name," the Prince was saying, "but you do not look in the least Russian."

"My mother .. thought it was a very .. pretty name," Katerina replied quietly.

She wondered what the Prince would say if she told him she had been born in St Petersburg. It is something he must .. never know, she thought quickly.

As if the Prince knew instinctively that she was not going to tell him any more, he did not press her. Instead he tapped with his gold-tipped walking cane against the glass window of the carriage. The horses came to a standstill and the footman jumped down.

"We are now ready to drive to the Villa Blanc by the Bois de Boulogne," the Prince said. "It is where we went yesterday." The footman nodded and shut the door.

The Prince turned to Katerina and asked: "If you are not Russian, then what nationality are you?"

"I am English," Katerina answered.

"I thought you must be," the Prince answered, also

speaking in English, "but I have never before met an Englishwoman who looked as lovely as you. In fact I thought with your fair hair that you might be Swedish."

"Your English is excellent," Katerina exclaimed.

"As is your French," the Prince replied. "In fact we are obviously both very talented people!"

Katerina laughed. "I . . hope so."

It flashed through the Prince's mind that few foreigners spoke French as well as Katerina.

His English was fluent, but the intonation was sometimes wrong. Yet he spoke a number of other European languages perfectly, each one without an accent.

The horses were moving up the Champs Elysées. As they passed the entrance to the Rue St Cloud, Katerina saw a carriage turning down it. She was almost certain it belonged to the Duc. She had thought that her stepmother had not expected him this evening as they were to dine alone. Yet she might have arranged for him to come later and he had been too impatient to wait until then.

The mere idea of his wanting her was horrifying and it made her shiver. The Prince perceived this and quickly said: "What has upset you? I do not want you to be afraid."

"I . . am not afraid of . . you," Katerina said at once.

"Then let me promise you that I will protect you from anybody else," the Prince said. "You are so lovely, Katerina, that there must be many men pursuing you, and, if that is true, then I swear I will keep them away."

Katerina gave him a shy little smile. "You are very .. kind," she said, "and it is .. stupid of me to be .. so frightened."

"I think it is very sensible of you," the Prince contradicted, "and you must not be pressured into doing anything you do not wish to do."

"It is .. difficult .. very difficult," Katerina murmured.

She was thinking that her stepmother was her guardian and she had no money. It would be impossible therefore for her to return to England when she could not pay the fare.

Then she remembered that although all she possessed were the clothes she stood up in, round her neck was a pearl necklace. Her father had given it to her the previous Christmas.

"It belonged to your mother," he said in a voice which told her how much it hurt him even to speak of her. He had put the necklace into her hands and said: "One day, all the jewellery your mother owned will be yours, but for the moment I could not bear to see it, or that anyone, even you, my precious daughter, should wear it."

It was an effort for him to go on, but he said: "These pearls belonged to your mother when she was a girl. I gave her three larger strips of pearls in which she looked more beautiful than the rising sun. But she always meant you to have these as soon as you were old enough to wear them."

Katerina had kissed her father. Yet because she was very near to tears she had found it difficult to find the words to thank him.

He understood, and she had worn the necklace every day since.

How can I sell it? How can I part with anything which was Mama's? she asked herself. But she knew, if she was to return to England and find one of her relatives to help her, that was what she would have to do.

The Prince reached out and put his hand over hers. "Try to stop worrying," he said. "Whatever is upsetting you, or whoever is frightening you, cannot hurt you at this moment. We are going to a party, and I want you to enjoy yourself."

He smiled before he added:

"If you look so worried and unhappy they might think I have been cruel to you, I assure you no man who was a man would crush a butterfly."

Katerina gave a shaky little laugh. "If I were a butterfly," she said, "I would use my wings to escape, but unfortunately I shall have to walk!"

"Nonsense," the Prince said. "You will dance, and looking as you do, there will be a magic carpet that will sweep you away over the roof-tops and up to the stars that are waiting for you."

"That is a beautiful thing to say," Katerina answered. "Do you always talk like that?"

The Prince's eyes twinkled as he replied: "When I am with anyone as lovely as you, it is impossible to be anything but poetical."

Now Katerina's laughter was spontaneous, and once again her eyes were shining.

Looking at her the Prince thought it was impossible that she could be real. Who would believe that, after Lettice had been so unpleasant, he would find standing beside his carriage anything so exquisite?

Aloud he said: "I think, Katerina, that as you are a mystery to me you will want the party we are attending to believe you are an enigma." Katerina was listening and he went on: "They will be curious about you – of course they will – but I will tell them that you are the spirit of Saronia and you have come with the jewels to help me win the contest. When we have done so, you will disappear back into the Aladdin's cave from which you came."

Katerina gave a little exclamation. "That is a lovely tale," she said. "I am sure it will puzzle everybody, so that there will be no need to answer their questions."

"That is what I thought," the Prince said complacently, "and of course, no one could look more like a jewel than you."

Katerina clasped her hands together. "That is the nicest compliment anyone has ever paid me!"

"And of course you have had a great many," the Prince remarked.

She looked up at him. "Now you are asking me a question. As it happens, I have had very few compliments this last year since I grew up," she said.

Because she had been at school she had not been able to join her father as often as she wished. She had also been aware that in the one month she had been in Paris after leaving school and before her father's fatal illness, her stepmother had made every possible excuse to exclude her from joining the dinner parties and receptions that took place at the Embassy.

"Katerina must wait until she has made her début," she had said firmly, "and has been presented at Buckingham Palace."

"I appreciate what you are saying," Lord Colwin had replied, "and of course I will make all the necessary arrangements. Meantime, I want Katerina with me, and she is very like her mother."

This was exactly what his French wife already thought. There was a hard look in her eyes when she looked at Katerina.

If Lord Colwin had been more perceptive, he would have been aware that his new wife was extremely jealous of her stepdaughter. As it was, he accepted his French wife at her face value. He was not particularly concerned about her thoughts or feelings. She made an excellent hostess, being charming and properly diplomatic to those he entertained. English people found her delightful, and he asked for nothing more.

He knew without putting it into words that never again would he find the closeness and intimacy, not only of the body but of the mind, which he had enjoyed with his first wife.

Every time he looked at Katerina she reminded him of her mother. There was a softness in his eyes, and the manner in which he spoke to her was very revealing.

*　　*　　*

The carriage drew up outside a large, important-looking house overlooking the Bois de Boulogne.

The Prince got out first, holding his large jewel-box with one hand. Then he helped Katerina out with the other.

He knew as he touched her that she was nervous and he said: "Remember, you hold the honour of my country in your hands! We cannot be beaten by a small and unimportant German principality!" The way he spoke in English made Katerina laugh.

She held her head high as they walked into the house.

The servants looked surprised that she wore no wrap that they could take from her shoulders. The major domo preceded them across the hall and two footmen in livery opened the doors that led into a large reception room.

"His Royal Highness Prince Michel of Saronia!" the major domo announced.

There was a group of people at the other end of the room, clustered round the fireplace. A man detached himself from the rest and came towards the Prince.

"My dear Michel, it is delightful to see you!" he said, holding out his hand.

As he took it the Prince remembered too late that he had neglected to tell Katerina that they were dining with his Serene Highness Prince Charles of Monaco and that she must curtsy to her host. He was therefore surprised that, as the Prince turned to greet her, Katerina sank down in a low curtsy.

She had in fact remembered as soon as she saw him

that her father had spoken of Prince Charles, and she had seen pictures of him in the newspapers.

"Let me introduce Katerina," Prince Michel said. He was aware that Prince Charles, who was expecting Lady Lettice, was looking surprised.

"Lady Lettice," he went on, "is unfortunately not at all well this evening and Katerina, at very short notice, has been kind enough to come in her place."

"I am of course delighted to see you," the Prince said graciously to Katerina, "but have you no other name?"

"She is just 'Katerina'," the Prince said quickly, "and has come like a good fairy to save me from the humiliation of having to come alone. However, as she is perhaps a little young for your party, you will understand that she is incognito, or rather, as I have already told her, the spirit of Saronia, a jewel to show a jewel."

Prince Charles laughed.

"Your imagination is running away with you, my dear Michel," he said, "and I think only you could find anything so lovely to take the place of Lady Lettice. You must of course tell her how much I commiserate with her."

"I will do that," the Prince replied.

Katerina realised there was a hard note in his voice. She wondered who Lady Lettice was and why she had let him down. She thought she must be English as her Christian name was an English one, and wondered to which distinguished family she belonged.

Now the Prince was being greeted by the other

people present. He introduced her again as just "Katerina".

They reached a large, red-faced man who she knew, even before she heard his name, was Prince Fredrich of Heinburg.

In a very guttural manner he asked in French: "Am I to understand, Michel, that Her Ladyship has refused to accompany you?" The way he spoke made it sound as if his suspicions were aroused by Lady Lettice's absence.

Michel said sharply: "She is unfortunately indisposed, and Katerina has obliged me by coming in her place."

Katerina curtsied, but she thought that Prince Fredrich held her hand too tightly and for an unnecessary length of time.

"I am glad you are here, Mademoiselle," he said, "although you will be on the wrong side."

He spoke in such a guttural voice that Prince Michel thought Katerina would not understand. To his surprise, however, she replied: "That, of course, Your Royal Highness, remains to be seen, and it is never wise to anticipate who will be the winner in such an unusual contest."

"As you have said," Prince Fredrich replied, "we shall know the results later. Meantime I can only say that you would look very beautiful in the Heinburg jewels."

It was a heavy compliment. Katerina, however, smiled at him in a way which Prince Michel thought was very charming.

Then, in case she should spoil the effect she had made, he introduced her to several of the women. They were, however, only interested in attracting his attention.

Katerina realised she had never seen any of them before. But she was aware that they were not the sort of guests who would have been entertained at the British Embassy. These women were younger and very much smarter than the majority of those who had sat round her father's table. She also thought they were not at all the type of women her mother would have welcomed. She had the suspicion that they were in fact what were known as '*demi-mondaines*'.

Many of them were outrageously overdressed and overbejewelled. They glittered, gushed, and waved their hands in a manner that seemed to caress Prince Michel.

"I am backing you, *mon cher*," Katerina heard one of them say to the Prince, "and if you lose the contest you will owe me a great deal of money!"

"Then of course to avoid that catastrophe," the Prince replied, "I must win, and with Katerina's help, how can I lose?"

Katerina was aware that the woman did not seem to be interested in her. As they all clustered round the Prince she thought they were like bees round a honey-pot.

Then to her surprise Prince Fredrich was once again at her side. "Why have I not seen you before?" he asked. "I cannot really believe that Michel brought you from Saronia just to take part in this gathering here tonight."

Katerina could see the curiosity in his eyes. At the same time, there was an expression in them which made her think of the Duc. Instinctively she moved a little away from him.

Before she could answer his question, he said in a low voice which could not be overheard: "When this evening has finished I must find you again. Where are you staying?"

Now Katerina was frightened. She looked towards Prince Michel. As if he was aware that she needed him, he moved away from the women chattering to him and came to her side.

"I trust you have been introduced to everyone, Katerina," he said.

"I am quite prepared to do that if you are too busy, Michel," Prince Fredrich offered.

The way he spoke was obviously intended to be unpleasant, but Michel replied: "Thank you, but I am perfectly capable of taking care of Katherina myself, and of course you have your own duties to perform."

The two men's eyes met. Then abruptly, as if he was annoyed, the German Prince turned away.

"He is a tiresome man," Prince Michel said in English.

"I find him . . rather frightening," Katerina replied.

"I am here, sword in hand, to protect you!" Prince Michel said. "But I am afraid it is going to be a very difficult task."

He introduced her to two other men who were both French and who paid her elaborate compliments. She did not seem to be embarrassed by them.

The Prince thought she must be older and more experienced than she appeared. At the same time, even before dinner was announced, he was aware that everyone there was curious as to who she was. They were obviously wondering how he could have produced anything so beautiful whom no one had ever seen before.

The woman who was to wear Prince Fredrich's jewels was almost the last to arrive. She was a junoesque German with fair hair and blue eyes. She was conventionally good-looking in a chocolate-box way. But compared to Katerina she looked coarse and very ordinary, despite the fact that she was most elaborately gowned. She was heavily made up and wore a vulgarly lavish amount of jewellery.

As they sat down to dinner Katerina learned from the Frenchman on her right-hand side that Prince Fredrich's model was a popular actress at the theatre.

"It will cost His Royal Highness a pretty penny tonight because she will not be appearing. But he is absolutely convinced that he will win this contest."

"Why is he so certain that he will do so?" Katerina asked.

"Because it is impossible for a German ever to admit that anyone else can be victorious," the Frenchman replied. "Prince Fredrich has been the rival of your friend Prince Michel and has always lost where many pretty ladies are concerned. So he is determined to win this . . duel of jewels."

Katerina laughed at the last words which he had spoken in English.

"A duel of jewels," she repeated. "Surely that is something new? I have never heard of one taking place before."

"Nor have I," the Frenchman agreed, "but it gives us something to talk about. Then, as soon as the duel is over, no one will talk of anything but you!"

"Now you are being flattering!" Katerina replied. "However, I am certain everyone here will be concentrating on the diamonds, the rubies, and the pearls, and nothing else will be of any importance."

"If you believe that," the Frenchman said in English, "you have not been aware of how Prince Fredrich has been watching you."

After this it was impossible for Katerina not to look near the other end of the table where Prince Fredrich was sitting.

She was then aware that it was true that he was ignoring the two women who were on either side of him. One of them, naturally, was the actress from the theatre. Instead his eyes were on Katerina and there was the same expression in them she had disliked before. Prince Fredrich frightened her. She decided that as soon as the contest was over she would leave.

Then the question sprang up at her almost as if it was written in letters of fire on the walls: WHERE WILL YOU GO?

If she went home, the Duc might be waiting for her. Certainly her stepmother would overwhelm her with questions as to where she had been and what she had been doing.

What shall I do? What shall I do? she asked herself.

As if what she was feeling communicated itself without words to Prince Michel he turned towards her. "You are looking worried," he said, "and you promised you would try to enjoy yourself."

"I .. it .. is the Prince," Katerina said without thinking. "I feel he is .. going to .. make trouble because .. I am .. here when I should not .. be."

As she spoke she knew that was the truth. Her father would not have wanted her to meet the women on either side of Prince Fredrich who were laughing too loudly. They were also being very familiar with the men on their other side. She thought too that the compliments paid her by the Frenchmen were too fulsome and too familiar. She could not put it into words, but she had the feeling that if she had been with her father at the Embassy they would not have spoken so freely. They would have been more respectful towards her.

It all flashed through her mind.

Then as if the Prince understood, he said: "As soon as this ridiculous contest is over we will leave, and I will take you wherever it is you wish to go."

He did not have to wait for her answer. He could tell by the expression in her eyes that she did not know where this could be. Then he said very quietly, "Leave everything to me. As I have told you, I will protect you even from the most unpleasant red-faced dragon!"

Because of the way he spoke, it was impossible for Katerina not to laugh, and the light was back in her eyes.

Chapter Three

Prince Charles said he thought it was time that the competition took place.

"After all, that is why we are here," he said to his guests, "and you are all to put a cross on the paper so that your votes will be anonymous and no one can be reproached afterwards." He could not help as he spoke just glancing at Prince Fredrich. One or two people smiled. They knew quite well that, if there were any complaints, they would come from the German.

Prince Michel reached out his hand and drew Katerina to her feet. "Come along," he said, "I have to make you look dazzling!"

They walked from the drawing room and into a smaller room on the other side of the hall.

They were alone there and she knew that Prince Fredrich was taking his actress somewhere else. The Prince shut the door.

She saw that he had already put the large jewel-box he had been carrying down on a table.

He opened it and she gave an exclamation. Fitted into the centre, so that it could not move, was the most beautiful crown. It flashed in the light of the chandeliers so that it seemed alive.

"This is the crown worn by the ruling Princess of my country," the Prince said, "and as you see, it is conveniently made in the form of a tiara rather than a crown."

"It is lovely – perfectly lovely!" Katerina exclaimed.

Decorated entirely with diamonds, except for the large capochon of emeralds that encircled it, she thought it was the most attractive piece of jewellery she had ever seen.

"You are not superstitious about emeralds?" the Prince asked. He was remembering how disagreeable Lady Lettice had been about them.

"I was born in May, so they are my birthstone," Katerina replied.

The Prince thought that once again his good luck had not let him down. He removed several trays and Katerina saw there was a necklace of emeralds and diamonds, bracelets to match and also earrings.

"How can you possess anything so fantastic?" she exclaimed.

Then she thought that perhaps the Prince would think it a rude remark.

"I am not surprised that you are astonished," he said, "but, I believe that they were made originally for Catherine the Great of Russia."

"I shall feel like Katerina the Great when I am wearing them," Katerina smiled.

The Prince lifted the crown from the jewel-box.

Katerina saw there was a large gold-framed mirror on each side of the fireplace. She went to stand in front of one of them.

The Prince placed the crown on her head, standing behind her to do so.

Looking at her reflection she thought that nothing could be more impressive. She wanted to have a picture of herself wearing something so magnificent.

She set the crown firmly on her head so that it could not move. The Prince then added the necklace, fastening it at the back of her neck.

It was, Katerina thought, almost providential that she should have been wearing a white gown. It was fashionable, leaving her shoulders bare, and the front of the gown was low. White chiffon was draped round it. It was as if the gown had been designed especially to set off the magnificent necklace.

Finally, when she was wearing a bracelet on each wrist and earrings falling down either side of her face, she seemed to glitter dazzlingly.

Prince Michel looked at her. He knew that Lady Lettice was the toast of St James's, and one of the most admired women in England, but there was no doubt that Katerina looked even more beautiful.

"How can I have been so lucky," he asked Katerina in a deep voice, "as to have found you? I can only thank you, thank you, for saving me at the last moment, from what would have been an humiliating situation."

"I cannot believe that any woman exists who would not long to wear such magnificent jewels," Katerina remarked. She thought a little wistfully that the only jewellery she had left, now that she had run away, were the pearls that had belonged to her mother. But at least when she sold them, they would enable her to pay her fare back to England.

"If you are ready," Prince Michel said, "let us go back and stun them! I think, for the first time in his life, Prince Fredrich will have to eat humble pie."

Katrina crossed her fingers and held them up. "It is unlucky to speculate until the horse has passed the winning-post."

Prince Michel smiled. "I am completely confident," he said, "that the Gold Cup and the ten thousand francs are already in my pocket."

Because she was afraid she might disappoint him, Katerina sent up a little prayer that Prince Fredrich's choice would not outshine her.

She thought the contest was one which would have amused her father. Silently in her heart she begged him to help her so that she would not disappoint the Prince.

Prince Michel opened the door, and as he did so they saw the back of Prince Fredrich as he walked into the drawing room.

A moment later they heard a burst of applause. Prince Michel held out his hand to stop Katerina from going any further.

"Give them time to inspect Prince Fredrich's jewels which I am quite sure will be very gaudy. Nor does his model look in the least like you." As he spoke he was thinking that it would be impossible, even if he searched the whole world, to find anyone who looked as lovely in the crown jewels of Saronia as Katerina.

He realised something he had not noticed before, that there was a touch of green in her eyes. The emeralds accentuated it. In the same way the diamonds made her skin look even more white and transparent than when he had first seen her.

He wondered who she could possibly be. Why, with such beauty, had she not been acclaimed amongst the French? They were always infatuated with any woman who was outstanding.

How was it possible, looking as she did, that he should have found her standing alone in a street completely unattended? She has run away, he told himself.

He was intensely curious to know the reason. If there was one thing the Prince enjoyed it was a mystery.

The majority of his love-affairs ended because the woman in question was no longer a mystery. In fact she had become so familiar that he knew what she was going to say before she spoke.

At twenty-nine he had been told over and over again that it was time he married and had a consort to help him rule over his country. There were certainly always a number of women who were only too willing to share his throne. But he enjoyed those who were sophisticated and were married, or widowed like Lady Lettice.

He was determined not to marry until it could no longer be postponed if he was to beget an heir.

He had said crossly to his mother before he left for Paris: "There is plenty of time for me to have a dozen children and you know as well as I do, Mama, that I would be bored within a week with any of the dull young women you constantly parade before me."

"I know, darling, that they are not as glamorous as the women who amuse you in Paris, or in many other countries, for that matter," the Queen Mother replied. "But I am anxious that our country should not be sucked into the German Federation, but should remain independent."

Her voice was very moving as she added: "If anything should happen to you, there would be nobody to take your place. How could I bear to see everything of which your father was so proud swallowed up by people with whom we have no real affinity?"

"You are quite right, Mama," the Prince replied, "but give me time – I must have time!"

His mother had sighed. Then she said: "I have a very attractive candidate coming to stay in two weeks' time, so do not be away too long."

Prince Michel had thrown up his hands in horror. "Not another boring young woman, Mama!" he pleaded. "They have nothing to say of any interest. And the mere idea of kissing any of them makes me feel sick!"

His mother had laughed. However, the expression

in her eyes was very sad. She adored her handsome son, but she knew that sooner or later he would have to take a wife.

It was of tremendous importance to Saronia that he should have an heir to succeed him. Saronia could play quite an important part in the balance of power in Europe. So they could reasonably plead with Queen Victoria for help as many of their neighbouring countries had done. A queen, or a reigning princess, who was English was at this moment of tremendous importance to them because it meant her people were sheltered by the Union Jack.

Queen Victoria was well aware of this. Already over twenty of her relatives sat on the thrones of Europe.

However, Prince Michel was determined that when he did take a wife he would choose her himself.

Saronia had always been very independent where its reigning prince was concerned.

The Queen Mother, who was Greek, had fallen in love with her husband long before she knew that he was the ruler of a country. That he loved her was not surprising. She was very beautiful and also extremely intelligent. She came from an ancient Greek family. Her father was also one of the most distinguished and admired philosophers that Athens had known this century.

When she had married the reigning Prince of Saronia they had been ecstatically happy. She always believed that the reason her son was handsome and intelligent was because he was born of love.

After he had left she prayed that one day he would be as happy as she had made his father.

Waiting behind the half-closed door now, the Prince said to Katerina: "Now! Go in with your head held high and remember that for the moment you are a queen or, if you prefer, a princess, for whom these jewels were originally intended."

She flashed him a smile, then forced herself not to feel nervous. I must not be afraid of these people, she told herself. It is the jewels they will be looking at, not me.

She walked slowly and with the grace she had been taught at dancing lessons at school. But it was in fact natural to her.

The Prince opened the door into the drawing room. She passed him and moved under the light of the chandeliers which she knew would be shimmering on the jewels.

Prince Charles's guests were seated in a semi-circle and facing them were two pairs of chairs like thrones. Two of the chairs were already occupied by Prince Fredrich and his model wearing his crown jewels.

One glance at them told Katerina that they were very different from what Prince Michel had given her. The crown the actress wore was of gold and made in the traditional manner with red velvet surmounted by a cross of diamonds. Round the bottom of it heavily inset were rubies, emeralds and pearls. It was clearly more suited to a man than a woman, and it gave the actress an almost comic appearance.

Similar jewels were set in a heavy gold necklace which was something like a dog's collar. There were large over-heavy bracelets around her wrists, which could in fact have been elaborate handcuffs.

The jewels themselves were very impressive, and Katerina was to learn later that they had come from India. But their setting was far too hard, too heavy, and certainly unfeminine.

When Katerina appeared there was, for a moment, a silence as if the audience drew in its breath. Then as she dropped them a very graceful curtsy they began to applaud.

As she straightened herself, one man cried out: "Bravo!" and the others followed. Then the applause became overwhelming. There was no doubt who was the winner, and there was no need for a secret ballot. Prince Charles, however, insisted on one.

While the audience made their crosses on the cards they had in their hands, Katerina sat with Prince Michel on the other chairs facing Prince Fredrich.

Katerina had only to look at his face to realise that he was extremely angry, knowing he had been defeated. But the way he looked at her made her feel very uncomfortable.

The cards were collected and the Prince of Monaco had only to glance at them before he said: "Prince Michel of Saronia is the winner! We can only congratulate him and his very beautiful model and thank them for the pleasure they have given us in seeing such elegant jewels." There was a round of applause after he had finished speaking.

Then the servants were bringing in champagne so that the winners could be toasted.

Prince Michel received the ten thousand francs which Prince Fredrich passed over with a bad grace.

There was a bouquet for Katerina besides a little gold box as a souvenir of the evening.

Then the party clustered round her to admire the jewels she was wearing. Because she felt sorry for the actress, Katerina then walked across the room to tell her how much she admired the jewels she was wearing.

"Whatever anyone else thinks of them," she replied to Katerina, "I would not mind possessing a few of them."

"I could say the same thing!" Katerina replied and they both laughed.

The actress turned to speak to somebody else and a voice in Katerina's ear said: "I will give you some beautiful jewels if you tell me where I can find you." Katerina looked round and realised it was Prince Fredrich who had spoken.

She thought how unpleasant he looked and how insulting it was that he should speak to her in such a way. She therefore made no reply, but moved away to be nearer to Prince Michel.

He had been talking to an elderly man. As Katerina came close to his side he looked at her and said in a voice only she could hear: "Who has upset you?"

"I am not . . upset," she answered, "but I do not want to . . talk to . . Prince Fredrich."

"What did he say to you?" Prince Michel enquired.

"He .. offered me .. jewels," Katerina answered.

The Prince had the idea that she did not know at all what that entailed. He frowned and said angrily: "Have nothing to do with him! He is an unpleasant man and it would be a mistake for you to see him again after tonight."

"That is what I thought," Katerina said. "How soon can .. we leave?"

"As soon as you like," the Prince answered, "or at least in a few minutes. It would be rude to leave too quickly."

After he had spoken Katerina thought there was really no hurry as far as she was concerned. She had nowhere to go unless she went back to her stepmother hoping that she would let her in. She can hardly expect me to sleep on the pavement! she told herself.

At the same time she was not too certain. Her stepmother's anger could continue for a long time. She would bear a grudge when anyone else would have forgotten what had happened.

"You are looking worried," the Prince said, "and you promised me that you would try to enjoy yourself."

"I am enjoying being here .. I am, really!" Katerina answered.

She could not help glancing round just to see if Prince Fredrich was anywhere near her. She had a feeling he was menacing her in the same way as the Duc was. There was no one to help or advise her. Once again she was thinking bitterly how lost she was without her father.

The champagne was flowing after they had drunk Prince Michel's and Katerina's health. A number of the party were becoming noisy and their laughter seemed to be unceasing.

The Prince decided it was time to leave. Going up to their host he said: "I think you will understand that now the excitement is over I should take my very alluring model home."

"Of course, Michel," Prince Charles replied, "and thank you for providing such an excellent 'Cabaret' turn. It was very kind of you to bring your jewels to Paris."

"It has been great fun," Prince Michel answered, "and I am delighted to be the winner."

He was thinking that it served Prince Fredrich right to lose a wager he should never have made in the first place. It had all arisen because he had been so bumptious and boastful about his crown jewels.

It had been impossible for Prince Michel to resist challenging him. The crown jewels of Heinburg were certainly, as Prince Fredrich had claimed, of great value and of unusual size.

At the same time, Katerina had made it impossible for anyone not to be overwhelmed by the exquisite picture she made.

The Prince said goodbye to one or two of his friends and Katerina thanked Prince Charles. She curtsied very prettily as she bade him good night.

They had reached the door when one of the women guests caught hold of Prince Michel and kissed him. "You have not been to see me for a long time, *mon cher*," she complained. "I will be waiting – you know I will be waiting – for you to call."

There was an insistent note in her voice which told Katerina how much it meant to her.

She was just thinking that the lady in question was very pretty when Prince Fredrich was beside her.

"I have to see you again, you beautiful siren!" he said in his guttural voice. "Tell me where you are staying, or I swear I will knock on every door in Paris until I find you."

Katerina gave a little laugh and would have moved away. But he reached out and took her by the hand.

"I want to see you again," he said, "I *must* see you, even if I have to fight Prince Michel for his jewels to do so."

"I hope you will not do anything so stupid," Katerina answered.

She tried to release her hand away from him as she spoke, but the Prince would not release it.

Without really thinking she added: "It would be a mistake to challenge him in case he beats you again." As she spoke she saw the anger in the Prince's eyes and wished she had remained silent.

"I do not speak lightly," Prince Fredrich said angrily, "when I tell you that I would kill Prince Michel to see you, and it is something I would not hesitate to do!"

There was something menacing in the way he spoke which made Katerina feel sure he really meant it. She pulled her hand away from him and without speaking ran out of the room.

Prince Michel, who had not heard what was being said, looked round in surprise, then followed her.

Katerina was waiting for him in the hall.

As he approached her he told a footman to bring his jewel-case from the sitting room. As the man hurried to obey he said to Katerina: "What is it? What has upset you now?"

"Prince Fredrich . . said he would . . kill you if you . . tried to prevent him from . . seeing me."

To her surprise Prince Michel laughed. "Boasting again," he said. "He always throws his weight about, and is surprised when nobody is impressed by him."

The footman came back carrying the jewel-case. Another footman had called for the Prince's carriage. He helped Katerina into it and as they drove away he said:

"Do not be upset. With any luck, if the Prince tries to find you he will fail. He invariably behaves disgracefully in one way or another, and I am delighted that, with your help, I beat him tonight."

"Does it really matter to you so much?" Katerina asked.

The Prince thought for a moment. Then he said: "No, you are quite right. It was stupid of me to accept his challenge when he said that he owned the best crown jewels in Europe."

He put out his hand to take hers before he went on: "I will always be deeply grateful that by chance I met you, and no one could have looked more beautiful. Even if a goddess from Olympus had been competing in the competition, you would still have been the winner."

Katerina gave a little laugh. At the same time she felt shy at what he was saying.

Then Prince Michel asked: "What am I to do about you?"

"I .. do not .. know," Katerina replied. "Perhaps I could .. stay at an .. hotel."

"Stay at an hotel on your own?" the Prince exclaimed. "Is it not possible for you to return to where you came from?"

Katerina did not answer and he said: "Please let me help you. If you will not tell me what the difficulty is, I find it impossible to understand how anybody as lovely as you should apparently be alone in the world, with no one to protect her."

There was a little pause. Then Katerina said: "I .. ran away because .. I was being forced by my stepmother to .. marry a man I .. dislike and who is .. old and horrible!"

"Then of course, if you feel like that, you must not marry him," the Prince said positively.

"It is very, very difficult for me to refuse .. and I am afraid .. if I go back .. I will be .. forced .. by one means or another to .. accept him."

Her voice was low and very frightened and the Prince said angrily: "It is disgraceful that you should be in such trouble, and of course I must save you."

Katerina's eyes lit up. "You will? But .. how?"

"That is difficult," he said, "but for tonight, at any rate, I think the only answer is for you to come back to where I am staying." His voice was serious as he went on: "At the same time you must realise that if anybody knew you were with me it could ruin your reputation."

He could tell even in the darkness of the carriage that Katerina was puzzled. He found it hard to believe that she was so innocent.

Then she said slowly: "I think if my father were alive, he would prefer me to risk my reputation than to be married to a man I hate . . and would rather . . die than be his wife."

There was no doubt that she was speaking with complete sincerity, and the Prince said: "In that case, we will take the risk and only hope that nobody finds out."

When he got into the carriage he had not told the coachman where to go. Now, as he tapped on the window with his walking-cane, the horses came to a standstill at the top of the Champs Elysées. The footman got down and opened the door.

"Where do you wish to go, Monsieur?" he asked.

"Back to the Rue St Honoré," the Prince answered.

The carriage started off again and he said: "I am staying at the house of a friend of mine, the Vicomte de Noade, but he and his wife are not in Paris, so I am there alone. Tomorrow I must think of somewhere else where you can go, or I will find somebody to chaperone you. But at least you can sleep tonight without being afraid."

"Oh, thank you . . thank . . you!" Katerina cried.

"You are so kind! How can I have been so . . fortunate as to have found a . . friend like you?"

The Prince thought with a little twinkle in his eyes that most women would have thought it very strange that she should trust him so completely. It was certainly not his usual reputation where anyone so beautiful was concerned. At the same time he felt that Katerina was little more than a child.

She had no idea of the problems and dangers she might encounter if she wandered about Paris alone. Nor in such circumstances as these, if she entrusted herself to a stranger. He was well aware that Prince Fredrich would have behaved in a very different way. So would the majority of the other men this evening.

He wondered who Katerina could possibly be, and found it difficult even to guess. She was obviously a lady, and yet no lady would have been alone on a pavement in Paris, of all places.

That she was innocent, unspoiled and completely pure positively vibrated from her. Therefore the Prince knew that because she trusted him he could not violate that trust.

When they arrived at the house where he was staying the front door was opened by a sleepy servant. After he had let the Prince and Katerina in he disappeared. He was obviously used to his master taking control of the proceedings at that time of the night.

The hall was well furnished and there was a beautifully carved staircase winding up to the next floor. The Prince took Katerina up it.

They walked past several closed doors until he opened one. It was used as a guest room and was next to the one he himself occupied.

When he lit the candles he saw that the bed was made with linen sheets edged with lace. The curtains were drawn and there was everything there that Katerina might want.

"You are quite safe here," the Prince said, "but if you are frightened, I am only next door. I will hear you if you call out to me."

"You do not . . think anyone will be annoyed with me," she asked, "for staying . . here without . . the owner's permission?"

"As I have told you, my friend is away. He always expects me to be his guest whenever I come to Paris, whether he is here or not."

"Then . . thank you once . . again," Katerina said. "I feel safe here and I know that no one will threaten me."

She was thinking not only of the Duc, but also of Prince Fredrich, as she spoke. The Prince was aware of this and it amused him, that she had not given a thought to the possibility that it might be himself who would frighten her.

"Go to bed, Katerina," he said. "You have played your part tonight more skilfully than anyone could have hoped, and I am very grateful."

She smiled at him.

He wanted to kiss her, but thought if he did so she would definitely be alarmed. If she should run away again into the street, there was no knowing what might happen to her. With what was an effort he turned towards the door.

"Goodnight, Katerina," he said, "and tomorrow everything may seem different."

"Thank you, thank you," Katerina said softly, "and if Papa were alive .. I know he would thank you .. too."

There was a little break in her voice which the Prince did not miss.

He walked out of the room closing the door behind him. As he went next door he knew that none of his friends would believe it. He had left the most beautiful woman he had ever seen untouched and unkissed, just because she trusted him.

When he got into bed he wondered whether perhaps he was being a fool and Katerina was deceiving him. Then he knew that no actress could have that childlike look in her eyes. No one could have pretended the fear that Katerina obviously was feeling when he first found her, or again when she recoiled from Prince Fredrich.

"I have to look after her," Prince Michel thought.

At the same time he mocked at himself for being a fool.

Katerina undressed and crept into bed wearing only her chemise.

She knelt first and said her prayers and thanked her father for looking after her.

"You have to help me, Papa, as you helped me tonight," she said. "Perhaps you sent Prince Michel to take me away before stepmama could drag me back into the house and hit me again because I would not agree to marry the Duc. But I cannot . . I cannot marry an old man like that! Oh, please . . go on helping me." She stifled a little sob. "If I can get to England . . I am sure there will be somebody with whom I can . . stay . . and who will not tell stepmama where I am."

She knew as she prayed that her stepmother would never give up her determination that she should marry the Duc. It would not only mean that she was provided for as his wife. She was also quite certain that the Frenchwoman would make sure that her own pocket was lined with gold. Then she would no longer have to worry about money as she was doing at the moment.

If her father were alive, Katerina was convinced, he would have sent the Duc away with a firm refusal. "If I go back there will be . . no one I can . . trust," Katerina told herself.

It was very comforting to know that Prince Michel, who had been so kind, was only next door. He would prevent anyone from intruding on her.

"I am lucky, so very, very lucky," she thought.

Then she fell asleep.

Chapter Four

Katerina stirred and realised that somebody was pulling back the curtains. For a moment she could not think where she was. Then she saw she was in bed and not wearing a nightgown.

A woman had come into the room, and after she had drawn back all the curtains she came to the bedside to say: "*Bonjour, m'mselle!* I have your breakfast outside."

"Oh, thank you," Katerina smiled. "I am afraid I have slept very late."

"It is past ten," the woman replied.

Katerina gasped, then as the woman came back with a tray in her hands she said: "I am so sorry to be so late, but I was very tired last night."

"That's what His Royal Highness said," the woman replied, "and he told me not to call you, *m'mselle*, until it was nearly time for you to dress." Katerina gave a little gasp and the woman went on: "His Royal Highness informed me that you've lost your luggage, so as soon as you've had your breakfast I'll find you something to wear."

"That .. is .. very kind .. of you," Katerina stammered.

"Madame la Vicomtesse is away just now, but she has left here most of the clothes she wears in Paris."

"Do you not think Madame would be .. annoyed at my .. wearing her clothes?" Katerina asked in a worried voice.

The elderly woman smiled and shook her head.

"I'm sure Madame would be only too pleased to be able to help you," she said. "At the moment she's having another baby, so I'm sure when Madame returns to Paris she'll want a complete new wardrobe."

Katerina looked surprised and the woman, who was obviously a gossip, went on: "Madame'll say to me, as she's said so often before: 'Marie, get rid of these old rags! I want everything new and in the latest fashion!' " The woman seemed to mimic the voice of the Vicomtesse, then went laughing from the room.

Katerina sat up and ate her breakfast. She thought it was very kind of Prince Michel to take such pains over her.

She decided that having escaped from her stepmother and the Duc she must somehow get to England.

I will ask the Prince to sell my pearls for me, she thought. Then once I am in England, I am sure that one of Papa's friends will help me, at least to hide so that stepmama cannot find me. It was a comforting thought.

At the same time she dreaded the idea of travelling alone, which was something she had never done before. When she had travelled with her father and mother there had always been couriers to look after them. There would be secretaries, lady's-maids, valets. If they were on diplomatic visits, there would be aides-de-camp to escort them.

"I can manage by myself," she nevertheless told herself confidently.

She had finished her breakfast when Marie came back to take away the tray. Then she brought in several gowns for Katerina to choose from. They were all extremely smart and in the latest fashion, and so attractive it was hard for Katerina to make a choice.

Finally she picked one of very pale spring green which reminded her of the beautiful emeralds she had worn last night. It was a gown with a little bolero jacket to wear over it. There was also a hat trimmed with green feathers. She thought it made her appear older and more responsible.

Marie was just putting the finishing touches to her hair when the old butler, who was Marie's husband, came up the stairs to say: "His Royal Highness is back, m'mselle, and waiting for you downstairs."

"He's taking you out to luncheon, m'mselle," Marie explained, "and I hope you go somewhere smart where people will admire you."

Katerina hoped she would do nothing of the sort, but she did not say so.

Surprisingly the Vicomtesse's gown was only a little loose for her round the waist, but otherwise it fitted her perfectly. The bolero might have been made for her. All it needed was some jewellery to create the right impression and she was glad she had her pearls.

She thought with a little pang that she would soon have to part with them. It meant losing the last link with her mother. But anything was better than having to marry the Duc.

"*Vous êtes très jolie*, m'mselle," Marie said approvingly as Katerina rose from the dressing table.

"Thank you for being so kind," Katerina answered.

"I will have something else for you to wear this evening when His Royal Highness takes you out to dinner," Marie promised.

Katerina thought that by that time she might be leaving for England. But there was no point in saying so.

She went downstairs slowly. She was feeling a little shy at having stayed last night in the house of a complete stranger and having borrowed clothes from a lady she had never met.

Prince Michel was waiting for her in a very attractive reception room. When she entered he did not speak, but just watched her as she walked towards him.

"Very smart, and absolutely perfect! Exactly how I expected you would look!" he said as she reached him.

Katerina smiled shyly. "It was very kind of you to arrange that I had something to wear," she said. "At the same time .. I feel embarrassed at imposing on you and of course on Madame la Vicomtesse, whom I have never met."

"Leave everything to me," the Prince said, "and now I am taking you out to luncheon."

Katerina was just about to say that she hoped it was nowhere smart, when he went on: "As I thought it would be a mistake for us to be talked about – and everybody in Paris does talk – I am taking you somewhere very quiet."

"I am glad about that," Katerina answered quickly. "It is what I hoped you would say, but I did not want to be .. a bore."

The Prince smiled. Then he said: "Now you are fishing for compliments. Come along and we will talk about everything while we eat the best food in Paris."

The carriage was waiting outside and they drove off.

It took a little time but the horses finally came to a standstill in a narrow street.

The restaurant did not appear at first glance to be of any importance. Inside, however, it was very well furnished and the way the Prince was greeted by the proprietor told Katerina he had often been there before.

They were given a comfortable sofa table in a corner at the far end of the room where they could see rather than be seen.

There was a long consultation with the proprietor over what they should eat. Katerina knew that the Prince would be far better at choosing the menu than she would. Finally, after what seemed an incredibly long time, everything was decided.

As the proprietor hurried away the Prince said: "That is one problem solved. Now we can get down to yours."

Katerina laughed. "Papa said that the French always take their food very seriously and approach it not only intelligently, but devoutly. But you are not French!"

"But I am a gourmet," Prince Michel said, "and in Saronia my people are gradually beginning to be as appreciative of haute cuisine as I want them to be."

"I am sure they follow everything you do and want to please you," Katerina said.

"That is what I hope," the Prince replied, "but, as you know, there are many problems in small principalities, and they are so afraid of being swallowed up by the greater powers."

Katerina had heard her father talk about that, but she thought it would be a mistake to appear to be too knowledgeable. Instead she asked: "Is your country beautiful?"

"Very beautiful," Prince Michel replied, "and we have some extremely fine horses, which I would like to see you ride."

"I can imagine nothing more wonderful," Katerina said, "but I want to ask you if you would be very, very kind and help me to get back to England."

"I think that is a sensible idea," the Prince said, "for, of course, there you will have relations and friends who will look after you and protect you from what is frightening you so much at the moment."

"If you could help me, it would be marvellous of you," Katerina answered. "So, please, could you sell my pearls for me?" She touched them as she spoke and thought she would miss them more than it was possible to put into words when she no longer felt them round her neck.

"Your pearls?" the Prince exclaimed. "Have you no money without doing that?"

"None," Katerina said, "just as I have no clothes. When you found me, I had left everything I possess behind."

The Prince was silent for a moment. Then he said: "Then of course I will help you, but I do not think you should travel to England alone."

"It is something I have . . never done before," Katerina admitted, "but I am . . grown up now . . and must learn to manage on my own."

The Prince looked at her as if he thought she did not really understand what she had said. Then he said softly: "There must be a better solution to your problem than running away."

"There is nothing, absolutely nothing I can do! But . . somehow I must reach . . England," Katerina said quickly.

"Of course. I must accept that you understand your situation better than I do," the Prince said reluctantly. "However, I am worried about you, Katerina."

He paused before he said slowly as if he was talking to himself: "You are so young and so lovely. You are certain to get into trouble sooner or later."

"I shall be .. all right in England," Katerina said confidently.

The first course arrived and because it was delicious they ate almost in silence. There was also a wine to drink which Katerina thought was like nectar.

When the plates were taken away the Prince said: "While we are eating what is some of the best food in Paris, I want to talk of things which will make you happy. So let us forget for the moment that you have to go to England, sell your necklace and – leave me."

There was a little pause before the last two words, and Katerina said quickly: "You have been so kind. I thought when I was saying my prayers last night how grateful I am that you appeared at exactly the right moment and saved me."

She remembered the man who had looked at her in a strange fashion when she was standing on the pavement. She thought it was not only from her stepmother that the Prince had saved her, but from other dangers too.

Prince Michel put out his hand and laid it over hers. "I want to help you, Katerina," he said, "but I feel handicapped from doing so." He spoke so emotionally that she looked at him in surprise. Then when she thought he would explain, the next course arrived and the Prince was explaining to her exactly what it was.

They then talked of Paris and of the Exhibition which had taken place the previous year at which the Prince had been present. Only when the meal was ended and they were sipping their coffee did Katerina feel they should talk about her return to England.

"I think," she said a little tentatively, "that it would be best if I went tomorrow morning, unless you would prefer me to go tonight?"

"I would prefer you never to go!" the Prince replied. "But I have to return to my own country, and amongst other things to take back as quickly as possible the crown jewels."

"I think Prince Fredrich was very angry at being the loser," Katerina said, "but compared to yours, his jewels were very ordinary, and too heavy to be becoming to a woman."

"While mine might have been made for you," the Prince said. "What I am going to do this afternoon is to take a photograph of you wearing them."

Katerina gave a little cry. "You have a camera?" she asked. "I have always been interested in them, but thought they must be very complicated."

"I have had mine for two years," the Prince replied. "It is the very latest and one which I feel will make you look as beautiful as in fact you are."

"No one could feel anything but beautiful wearing your magnificent emeralds and diamonds," Katerina answered.

"Some people are superstitious about emeralds," Prince Michel replied, thinking of Lady Lettice. He had no intention of seeing her again and he thought how angry she would be at his absence.

She had come to Paris especially to be with him.

He had been thrilled and delighted by her until he found how difficult and petulant she could be. He knew it was because she had been spoilt by so much adulation.

He was used to women who allowed him to make all the decisions and did not assert themselves unnecessarily. When he thought about it, he realised that the women who attracted him were naturally soft, gentle and very tender. This was because the Saronians as a nation were fighting men. They had proved themselves over the centuries by managing to remain independent. This despite the fact that most of the countries which surrounded them were large and aggressive.

A Saronian woman could only get her own way by coaxing and keeping her man so infatuated with her that he was prepared to give her everything she wanted. They had the spirit of the Hungarians and rivalled them as equestriennes.

The Prince thought there was nothing he wanted more than to see Katerina riding one of his spirited horses. He was quite certain she was a good rider. Just as he knew that if he danced with her it would be as if they were dancing on clouds. When she was in his arms he knew she would be as light as the wind.

"What are you thinking about?" Katerina asked a little nervously. "Have I . . said anything . . wrong?"

"No, of course not," Prince Michel assured her. "How could you do anything that was wrong? Everything about you is perfect from the top of your head to the tips of your toes!"

Because there was a note in his voice that she had not heard before she blushed and he said: "Now you are like the dawn sweeping through a sable sky. Oh! my dear, how can I lose you?"

She looked at him in surprise, then her eyes flickered and she blushed again.

"I have to let you go," Prince Michel said, "and it is the hardest thing I have ever done in my life."

He knew Katerina did not understand. But he also knew it was impossible to tell her that as she was a commoner he could not offer her marriage. Because he was well aware of her purity and innocence, he could not shock her by asking her to be his mistress.

"I will take you back to the house," he said abruptly.

Quickly, as if she was embarrassed, she started to pull on her gloves. The Prince paid the bill, then he walked to the door.

Just as the carriage, which was waiting a little further down the street, started to drive towards them the Prince gave an exclamation. "I have left my cane in the restaurant," he said. He did not wait for Katerina to reply, but turned and walked back into the restaurant.

The carriage was now approaching. As Katerina waited for it she was aware of another carriage coming from the opposite direction. Because of the narrowness of the street it had to pull in its horses.

Unexpectedly the carriage-door opened and a man jumped out and came across the road towards her. She glanced at him casually, then realised that it was Prince Fredrich.

"So here you are!" he exclaimed unnecessarily as he reached her. "I have been looking for you, searching for you, and wondering where you could possibly be."

"You . . wanted me?" Katerina asked in surprise.

"Of course I wanted you!" the Prince asserted. "I thought I had made that clear before you left Prince Charles's house. I will give you everything you want if you come with me – far more than young Michel could give you – and I am sure he would not be allowed to take you to Saronia."

Katerina stared at him in astonishment, not understanding what he was saying.

Then he moved even closer to her and said in an insistent voice: "I will take you to Heinburg with me. I will give you a house, a carriage and horses of your own, and jewellery in which you will look magnificent!"

Katerina gasped.

At that moment Prince Michel came out of the restaurant carrying his cane. He took one look at Prince Fredrich and scowled.

"How have you managed to turn up here?" he asked.

"That is my business," Prince Fredrich retorted. He turned to Katerina. "I meant what I said and I shall be waiting for your answer." With that he walked away and got back into his carriage just as the Prince's horses stopped beside them.

A footman jumped down and opened the carriage door. Katerina got in and as the Prince joined her he asked: "What was that red-faced German saying to you?"

He spoke so angrily that Katerina thought it would be a mistake to enlighten him. She was afraid it would make more trouble between the two Princes than there was already.

"He was just saying that he wanted to . . see me," she answered. "Fortunately he does not know where I am, for I want nothing more to do with him."

"You are right there," Prince Michel agreed.

As the horses drove on he put his hand over hers. "Now, listen, Katerina," he said, "I have to go now to a meeting with the French Secretary of State for Foreign Affairs which I cannot cancel. I will get away as quickly as I can. Then we can decide what we will do this evening."

"You do not mind if I stay for another night?" Katerina asked shyly.

"Of course you must stay with me," the Prince said, "and tomorrow we will talk again about your going to England. But I cannot allow you to travel alone."

Katerina gave a little sigh. She thought he was going to suggest that she had a courier, but she knew they were expensive. At the same time she was sure it was what her father and mother would have wanted. Therefore she must try to do what was right.

She wondered how much the Prince would get for her pearls. It might have to last for a very long time, so she must economise in every way possible.

There was also, although she did not like to mention it, the difficulty of clothes. She wondered if perhaps she could buy from Marie what the Vicomtesse had already discarded. If not, she would have to patronise a cheap shop before she left for England.

It was all passing through her mind, but at the same time she had no wish to trouble the Prince. She knew he was extremely annoyed that Prince Fredrich had found her and had been talking to her.

She tried tactfully to make him forget it by talking of the places of interest they were passing. When they reached it the beauty of the Place de la Concorde was breathtaking.

The horses stopped outside the Vicomte's house and the Prince helped her out before he said: "I will be as quick as I can, but I am afraid it is an important conference, and may last several hours."

"Do not worry about me," Katerina replied. "I saw there were books in some of the rooms, and I shall be quite content if I can read them."

"I am glad about that," the Prince replied. "But miss me a little, otherwise I shall be jealous, even of the books!"

Katerina laughed, thinking he was just paying her a compliment. She had no idea that as he drove away he was asking himself desperately: "What the devil can I do about her? Oh, God, how can I lose her?"

Katerina ran upstairs to take off her hat and Marie followed her into her room.

"Did you have a good luncheon, m'mselle?" she enquired.

"Every mouthful was a poem in itself," Katerina replied.

Marie laughed. "We French like to cook, but the English only like roast beef and apple pie, while the Germans like sauerkraut. I am always glad, so very glad, that I am French!"

"I am sure you are," Katerina smiled.

Marie helped her out of her jacket. "I have a gown for you, m'mselle, in which you will look *très belle* for when Monsieur le Prince returns."

Katerina wanted to expostulate that there was no need for her to change. However, when she saw the gown she could not resist it. It was a lovely afternoon gown in a very pale blue with touches of pink so subtly interwoven in it that she looked exactly like a flower.

"Are you quite certain that Madame la Vicomtesse will not mind my wearing this?" she asked.

"Madame has had this gown for nearly two years," Marie answered. "She will never wear it again, of that I can assure you."

"It is lovely, completely lovely!" Katerina said. "Thank you, Marie, for lending it to me!"

Marie hesitated a moment, then she said: "Madame told me to dispose of it, but like her evening gowns it is too smart, too elegant for anyone I know."

"Then perhaps . . I could . . buy some of them?" Katerina said hesitatingly. "I think His Royal Highness is arranging for me to have some money with which to return to England, but I am sure there will be enough left over for me to buy this beautiful gown from you, and perhaps a few more."

Marie smiled all over her face. "That is an arrangement between you and me, m'mselle," she said, "and we are both satisfied."

"Yes, of course," Katerina agreed. She thought, however, that she must tell the Prince in order to make sure she was not doing anything wrong. It would be terrible if, after all his kindness to her, she offended his hostess and made what her father would have said was a shocking *faux pas*.

Marie managed to talk until the very last moment before Katerina ran down the stairs to the drawing room. She saw there were no bookcases amongst the very elegant furniture there. So she went next door to a room of which she had only a quick impression before. Now she was aware that she was right in thinking there were a number of books there.

They were enclosed in a number of glass-fronted bookcases.

She opened the first case and found a number of books in French, some of which had just been published. They were all by the most famous French authors, whose names she had seen in the bookcases in the British Embassy.

Now, she told herself, she had at least two hours before the Prince returned.

She chose a book by Dumas which was one she had wanted to read.

Sitting down on a comfortable sofa she raised her legs and opened the book. Over two hours had passed and she was deep in it, fascinated by the way he wrote.

Suddenly the door opened and Anton, who was Marie's husband, announced: "His Royal Highness Prince Fredrich of Heinburg, m'mselle."

Katerina started and looked round in consternation to see Prince Fredrich approaching her. He was looking, she thought, even more unpleasant than he had earlier in the day.

"At last I have found you!" he said. "I did not believe at first that Michel would dare to bring you here! I cannot think what Madame la Vicomtesse would say about it!"

"I do not know what you are talking about," Katerina said coldly.

She moved her legs from the sofa, but she did not rise, as she knew she should have done to curtsy to the Prince.

"Anyway, that is none of my business," he went on. "What I am concerned about, Katerina, is you. Have you thought over what I said outside the restaurant?"

"I am not in the least interested in anything you say," Katerina replied. "And let me inform you that I am leaving for England tomorrow."

"How can you think of doing anything so absurd?" the Prince blustered. "You know I will give you everything you want – and a great deal more!"

He sat down beside her on the sofa and said: "I am infatuated with you! The moment I saw you I knew that nothing could be more attractive, and that I had to make you mine!"

Katerina moved a little way away from him. "Your Royal Highness is mistaken," she said. "I belong to no one but myself, and I am returning to England to be with my relatives."

The Prince laughed, but it was not a pretty sound. "I was wondering if you have a Protector in London. But he could not give what I can give you – as I have already said – your own house, a carriage, horses, and pearls and diamonds which will make you glitter even more brilliantly than you do already!"

Because he was bending towards her as he spoke, Katerina was frightened by the expression in his eyes. She got quickly to her feet.

"I think, Your Royal Highness," she said, "you are insulting me. I want nothing you can offer me and am quite capable of looking after myself!"

The Prince laughed again, but this time it was scornfully. "So you are playing hard to get!" he said. "Well, I do not blame you but, let me tell you, you do not deceive me. You are Prince Michel's mistress, and you are staying here without an invitation from the lady of the house who would, I assure you, be extremely annoyed if she knew about it."

For a moment Katerina could only stare at him in sheer astonishment. Then she said furiously: "How dare you suggest that I am the mistress of Prince Michel! He is a friend – do you understand? – just a friend who has been kind to me when I needed help. If my father were alive, he would be enraged by your allegation!"

The Prince rose to his feet. "If you are not Michel's

mistress," he said, "that is certainly something that pleases me. I want you, Katerina, and I intend to have you myself."

He moved quicker than she expected and swept her into his arms. She gave a cry that was one of surprise. Then, as he tried to kiss her, she struggled violently against him. She managed to avoid his lips but she felt them pressing against her cheek. His arms were like bands of steel round her body.

She screamed and suddenly the door opened and she heard Prince Michel's voice. "What the devil's going on here? Leave her alone, you swine!"

Prince Michel grabbed Prince Fredrich by the back of his collar so that he released his hold on Katerina and she managed to scramble away from him.

She saw Prince Michel hit the German with all his force on the chin. He staggered and would have fallen to the ground had he not collapsed into a chair with one leg over the arm.

"How dare you strike me!" he demanded furiously in German.

"Get out!" Prince Michel said violently. "I did not invite you here. How dare you upset Katerina and force your obnoxious attentions upon her!"

Prince Fredrich spluttered and Prince Michel said again: "Get out and stay out! If I find you here again I will challenge you to a duel! I can assure you I am a damned sight better shot than you are!"

As if Prince Fredrich knew this was true, he muttered to himself as he got out of the chair. He walked towards the door and only as he reached it did he look back as if he wanted to insult Prince Michel. Then as if he thought better of it, he went from the room.

Only as the door shut noisily behind him did Prince Michel turn round. As he did so, Katerina flung herself against him.

"You saved me! You saved me!" she cried. "He is horrible! Insulting! Disgusting! I was so . . frightened . . so very . . frightened!" The words seemed to tumble over themselves and the Prince held her very close.

"It is all right, my darling," he said, "he will not hurt you again."

Then, as she looked up at him, her eyes wide and still frightened, he bent his head and his lips found hers.

Chapter Five

For a moment Katerina could not think what was happening.

Then the pressure of the Prince's lips made her feel as if the sunshine had suddenly invaded her body. Her whole being seemed to come alive. He kissed her for a long time and finally, when he raised his head, she said: "I .. I did not .. know that a kiss could be .. so wonderful!"

"It is wonderful if you love somebody," the Prince said in a tender tone, "and I love you, my darling, as I have from the first moment I saw you." Then he was kissing her again, possessively, but gently, as if she was infinitely precious.

Then he said: "This should never have happened! I did not mean it to happen."

She looked at him in surprise. "Why?" she asked. "It is wonderful .. marvellous! How could I have .. known that .. love could be like this?"

As she spoke Katerina knew this was what she had always sought and what her father and mother had known. It was what she had prayed she would find.

Then, to her surprise, the Prince took his arms from her and walked across the room. Because her legs felt unsteady she sat down on the sofa watching him.

"What can I say to you? What can I do?" he asked finally.

"W . . what have I . . done wrong?" Katrina asked miserably, and it was the cry of a child.

The Prince sat down beside her and took her hand in his. "You have done nothing wrong, my precious, you were perfect, absolutely perfect. I love you, but I have tried not to tell you so."

"But . . why . . why?" Katerina asked. "I love you . . but I did not know that what I was feeling was love . . I just knew that I could . . trust you and that you are the most marvellous man I have ever met."

The Prince squeezed her hand so tightly that it hurt. "You are not to say such things to me," he said, "it only makes things harder."

"Harder for . . what?" Katerina asked.

"For me," the Prince said, and suddenly his voice was very harsh.

There was a little silence. Then Katerina replied: "But you know I have to . . leave you . . I have to go to England . . and I think I will be . . safe there."

The Prince rose again to his feet almost as if he could not bear to touch her. "How can I let you go to England alone?" he asked. "I found you in the street, and because you are the most beautiful person I have ever seen I protected you, but another man might behave very differently."

Katerina thought of Prince Fredrich and shivered.

"What did he say to you when I was in the restaurant?" he demanded.

Katerina blushed, then she said in a very small voice: "H .. he .. asked me to be his .. mistress .. I .. did not .. understand at first what he .. wanted. Then I realised that he was .. insulting me."

"Of course he was," the Prince said. "But you must understand, my lovely one, that if you go about alone looking as you do, it is what a great many men will suggest to you."

"Oh .. no!" Katerina cried in horror.

"That is why you must be escorted," the Prince said as if he was speaking to himself, "and no one must ever know that you stayed here alone with me."

"Prince Fredrich is aware of it," Katerina reminded him.

"Curse him!" the Prince cried. "The sooner he goes back to his own country, the better!"

He was just about to walk out of the room when he turned back again and said: "I will tell you what I will do – I will take you to England myself. But we cannot leave until the day after tomorrow."

"B .. but you do not want to .. go to England," Katerina said.

"I cannot allow you to travel alone," the Prince said sharply. "As I have just said, you must realise there will be men who, after one look at you, will want to possess you for themselves."

Katerina put her hands up to her cheeks as if she would cry. "I .. I am sorry," she said.

The Prince gave a little laugh. "How can you be sorry for being beautiful?" he asked. "You are the most beautiful person I have ever seen. Oh, my darling, my precious one, if only I could do what I want to do!"

Katerina clasped her hands together and looked at him curiously. "What .. do you want to do?" she asked.

"Never mind that now," he replied. "What we will do now is to change and go out to dinner somewhere where I can talk to you and look at you." He paused for a moment. Then he said as if he was working it out: "I will take you to see Paris by night. We will drive beside the River Seine and you will see the lights on the barges and on the bridges."

"I would like that," Katerina smiled.

"It will be something for us to remember," the Prince said. There was a pain in his voice Katerina did not understand. Only when he had kissed her very tenderly again and she had gone to her room did she ask herself why he seemed so unhappy.

I love him, she thought as she undressed, but I know he has to go back to his own country because, as Papa would have said, it is his duty.

She did not realise that the Prince was going through all the tortures of hell. He knew that he loved Katerina as he had never loved any woman before. But there was nothing he could do about it, and when he went back to Saronia he would never see her again. He did not want to think of what might happen to her or that men would pursue her. He only knew that to be apart from her would be an agony he had never before experienced with any other woman.

Katerina came downstairs wearing a very pretty gown that Marie had found for her. She had enjoyed a scented bath which she knew the French seldom had. Marie, however, had expected that, being English, she would want one.

She apologised to Marie saying: "I am sorry your husband has had to carry those heavy cans of water upstairs, but I do enjoy a bath before dinner, and my father always insisted on doing the same in every country to which he was posted."

"I knew it was what you'd want, m'mselle," Marie said in a tone of satisfaction, "and it wasn't as hard for my husband as you might think, although he's finding the stairs a bit of trouble because of his arthritis."

"That was what was worrying me," Katerina said in a soft voice.

"Well, he's engaged help," Marie explained. "A rather nice boy who says himself he's as strong as an ox, and can carry upstairs two of the big cans filled with water without any trouble."

"I am so glad about that!" Katerina said with relief.

"My husband knows as soon as His Highness returns he too'll be wanting a bath," Marie went on in her usual chatty way. "So I says to my husband, get someone in to help you, otherwise you'll be laid up and no use to anyone!"

"I think that was very sensible of you," Katerina said as Marie walked towards the door.

"Zerge might not be everyone's choice, seeing he's only half-French and has got a bit of colour about him – Algerian, I thinks it is. But he's strong and willing, and who wants more?" Marie continued.

"Who indeed?" Katerina murmured.

She was hardly listening to Marie. Only thinking of Prince Michel and how his kisses had been different from anything she had ever imagined in her dreams.

She had no idea she could feel so ecstatic. He seemed to sweep her up into the sky. Then nothing but Michel had been of any consequence, not even Prince Fredrich with his insults.

She wondered what her father would think. Yet she had to admit that it was her own fault for not telling anyone who she was. She was, in effect, putting herself on a par with Prince Fredrich's actress who had shown off his jewels. And with the other painted and over-dressed women at the party.

The sooner I get back to England, the better! she thought.

She decided it was no use worrying. She would go to one of her father's old friends and ask his help. She knew several of them whom she had met whenever they returned to England. She was quite sure, as they had been fond of her father, they would not press her to marry the Frenchman, even if he was a Duc.

They knew Mama, Katerina thought with satisfaction, and they will help me to behave as she did. At the same time, it was frightening.

She hoped that Prince Michel would not change his mind, but would take her to England, as he had said he would.

I must .. not impose .. on him, she told herself. Yet if he did take her, it meant she could be with him a little while longer.

She tried not to think of the moment when they had to say goodbye. She would never see him again.

The gown that Marie had chosen for her was really lovely. Made of tulle, it was a soft mauve, the colour of Parma violets.

When the Prince saw her coming down the stairs he could only stare at her for a long moment. Then he said: "How is it possible that every time I see you you are more beautiful than I remembered? I never thought of you wearing that particular colour, but you look even lovelier than you did last night."

"I am beginning to think that Marie is my fairy godmother," Katerina replied. "She waves her magic wand and I appear in another gown. I am only hoping that at midnight I do not suddenly find myself, like Cinderella, in rags!"

"You would still look beautiful in them!" the Prince said. He raised her hand as he spoke and kissed it.

At the touch of his lips she felt a quiver run through her and he was aware of it. For a moment he looked at her and she thought he was going to take her in his arms. Then he turned away and said abruptly:

"Come along. The horses are waiting, and I have thought of a charming place to take you where there will be music as a background for all the things I wish to say to you."

Katerina thought that sounded very romantic. As she got into the carriage she slipped her hand into his. "It is very, very exciting going out to dinner with you," she said. "I have never before been out alone with a man."

"And you had never been kissed by one," the Prince added.

"No . . of course . . not," she answered.

She heard him draw in his breath, but he did not say anything. His fingers tightened on hers and they drove on in silence.

The restaurant he had chosen to take her to was in a fashionable part of Paris. There were only two other people there when they arrived. Katerina wondered if the Prince had chosen it because it was not popular.

The music was provided by a piano very well played and a violinist. The music was soft. Katerina thought Prince Michel was right when he said it would make a background for what they said to each other. Or for what they did not say. There were moments of silence when they just looked into each other's eyes and spoke without words.

She knew that he loved her as she loved him. He is so handsome, she thought, so exciting! He must have dozens of women in love with him and when I have gone . . there will be dozens more! The thought was like a dagger in her breast!

Because she thought it would be boring to be dramatic or depressed, she tried to talk interestingly, just as she would have done with her father and his friends. But behind every word they said, behind every subject they discussed, was the overwhelming knowledge that they were close to each other. Nothing else mattered.

Gradually the restaurant was filling up as they ate. Katerina saw that most of the diners were older. They were also what her mother would have described as very respectable. The women were not painted, nor did they wear a great deal of jewellery. They were obviously ladies and the men who accompanied them were gentlemen.

She could understand that they appreciated the food perhaps more than younger people might have done. Every dish was a work of art.

Finally, as they were enjoying the dessert, two more people came in at the far door. Katerina glanced at them curiously. Then she made a little murmur and put her hand up to her face.

"What is it?" the Prince asked.

"I .. must leave," she whispered. "Take me away .. from here .. quickly!"

The Prince looked in the direction where she had looked. He saw a middle-aged, distinguished-looking man escorting a smartly dressed woman who was obviously French.

Then he said with a note of surprise in his voice: "That is the Duc de Soisson. Why should he upset you?"

"T .. take me .. away!" Katerina pleaded. "Please .. please .. take me .. away." There was a note of terror in her voice that the Prince did not miss.

He waited until the newly arrived couple were seated. It was fortunately at the opposite end of the room from them. Then he beckoned the proprietor to the table.

"I hope Your Royal Highness has enjoyed your dinner?" the proprietor asked.

"I have indeed," the Prince answered, "but my companion is feeling unwell. Have you a door through which we can leave without drawing attention to ourselves?"

The proprietor looked surprised. Then as if he understood he said: "But, of course, Monsieur."

The Prince rose and helped Katerina to her feet. Following the proprietor he drew her beside him towards a door which was not far from where they had been sitting. It was impossible for any of the other diners who looked in their direction to see anything but his back. Katerina was in front of him so that she was completely hidden.

The proprietor took them through a serving-door which led into the kitchen. A number of chefs were busy preparing the meals. On the other side there was a door which opened onto an alley.

As they reached it Prince Michel took some large notes out of his pocket. He put them into the proprietor's hand.

"But it is too much!" he protested.

"You can give me a credit for the next time I come!" Prince Michel smiled.

"Your Royal Highness is always welcome," the proprietor said, bowing.

The Prince hurried Katerina through the door. The alley was filled with dustbins which contained all the rubbish from the restaurant. They made their way to the road in which the carriage was waiting.

The Prince helped Katerina into it. She realised that, on his instructions, while they were in the restaurant the hood had been let down.

It was a warm night, the stars were coming out in the sky and the moon was rising. She knew he had planned that she should see Paris by moonlight.

She did not notice until they had driven away from the restaurant that there was a fur wrap on the opposite seat. Now the Prince put it round her shoulders.

She thought with a little sigh that he enslaved her as no one else would ever do.

As the horses quickened their pace he told the coachman to go slower. Taking her hand in his Prince Michel said: "Now you are safe, but, darling, you must tell my why you were so frightened of the Duc de Soisson and who you are."

"I .. will .. tell you .. everything," Katerina promised, "but if I tell you now it will spoil our evening together. Can we not just drive and look at Paris first, and I can think you are protecting me."

The Prince gave a little laugh and put his arm around her. "We will do exactly as you wish, my darling," he said. "This is an evening we will both want to remember, so we will forget everything but ourselves and the beauty of Paris, which moves us both." He kissed her hair as he spoke and Katerina moved a little closer to him.

She knew this was something she would always remember. She could not bear it to be spoilt by speaking of her stepmother, or of the Duc.

The Prince took her first to the Place de la Concorde where the fountains were throwing their water up into the sky. It glistened in a thousand rainbows as it splashed into the sculpted basins beneath it.

Then they were driving beneath the trees along the Seine. The lights were reflected in its water, as were the stars overhead. It was so beautiful, so moving that Katerina thought the scene would be engraved on her heart for ever.

They drove for some way, until on the Prince's instructions the carriage stopped. To Katerina's surprise he helped her out.

They walked down some narrow steps until they were on the narrow path which ran beside the river below the road. There was a bridge just ahead of them, and when the Prince drew Katerina under it he did not speak but took her in his arms.

Then he was kissing her, kissing her wildly, passionately, demandingly. It was as if he could no longer control his love for her and could only express it with his lips against hers. She thought the lapping of the river beside them was like music. The Prince swept her into the wonder of the night where all troubles and difficulties were left behind. They were in a paradise all their own.

"I love you!" the Prince said. "Oh, God, how I love you!"

He kissed her neck and it gave her a strange ecstatic

feeling that made her head turn a somersault. Then he kissed her lips until they were both breathless.

They had been standing for a long time under the bridge without saying anything. At last the Prince took Katerina by the hand and drew her back up the steps. She knew then that they had to come back to reality and she would have to tell him what she had kept hidden.

They drove back almost in silence.

Then, when they reached the Vicomte's house and were let in by Zerge, they went into the drawing room.

There was a bottle of champagne in an ice-cooler on a table in the corner of the room. The Prince poured out two glasses. Then when he had given Katerina hers he sat down beside her and said gently:

"Now, my darling, my precious love, you must tell me what I am so curious to know, and there must be no more secrets between us."

"You will .. still .. love me?" Katerina asked.

"How can you doubt that?" he asked. "I will love you from now until eternity."

Her eyes widened and she looked at him.

They were both very still until he said in a different tone that was somehow harsh: "Tell me the truth and let us get it over. If I kiss you again, I shall forget everything but you."

Katerina took a sip of the champagne, then put the glass down on a small table beside her. "My .. father," she said, "was Lord Colwin."

The Prince stared at her before he exclaimed: "The British Ambassador?"

"Yes," Katerina said. "As you may know, he died a short time ago .. and I was left with .. my stepmother."

The Prince was frowning as if he was trying to remember. But Katerina went on: "When my .. mother died my father was .. lonely and he needed someone to be hostess for him. So he .. married Madame Beauvais, who is of course French."

"I think I remember hearing that," the Prince said.

"We had to move out of the Embassy," Katerina went on, "and my stepmother took a house in the Rue St Cloud."

She knew by the expression in the Prince's eyes that he remembered that was where he had found her standing alone on the pavement. She went on quickly: "We had been there only a short time – not quite a month – when my stepmother informed me that the Duc de Soisson wished to marry me."

"Marry you?" the Prince exclaimed. "But he is old enough to be your father!"

"Yes, I know," Katerina replied, "and that is why I .. refused."

"Of course you did," the Prince said. "He is not only far too old for you, but he also has a very bad reputation."

"I hate .. him and the way he .. looked at me," Katerina said, "but, you understand, my stepmother is .. my guardian.

"Do you mean," the Prince demanded, "that as your guardian she is insisting that you marry the Duc?"

"She was . . furious when I . . refused," Katerina said hesitatingly, "and the . . night you found me . . she had told me that I would have to marry the Duc if she dragged me . . unconscious to the altar. Then . . she . . hit me . . and losing her temper . . pushed me out of the h . . house and l . . locked the door . . behind me."

The Prince stiffened as if he could hardly believe what he was hearing. Then he said: "Thank God I found you! So that is what happened and, my darling, you were right — of course you were right — you must never marry the Duc de Soisson or any man like him!"

"I was . . frightened that my . . stepmother would somehow force me to . . marry him," Katerina said, "and I was thinking . . I must run away so that they could not find me . . then you were there!" She smiled at him and the Prince thought it would be impossible for anyone to look more beautiful.

"I saved you," he said in a deep voice, "and that is what I must continue to do. My precious, my darling, you do realise that I cannot ask you to be my wife?"

"I . . know that . . you are . . royal," Katerina murmured.

"I am royal," the Prince said, "so if I married you it could only be a morganatic marriage. You would be ignored by my family and most of the nobility in my kingdom." He gave a deep sigh. "How could I ask you to suffer like that? On the other hand, how could I ask you to accept anything less than marriage?"

There was silence for a moment. Then Katerina said: "I .. understand .. of course I understand. Having lived with Papa, I know how .. important royalty are in their .. own country." There was a little sob in her voice as she spoke. "I know .. Mama and Papa would be very . . . shocked if they knew that men like Prince Fredrich had asked me to be their .. mistress."

"Forget him!" the Prince said angrily. "At least the Duc had the decency to offer you a wedding ring!" Putting out his hand he took Katerina's. "You are not to accept his offer – do you understand? I know a great deal about that man, and he could never in a million years be worthy of having you as his wife."

"That is .. what I .. felt," Katerina answered, "and why I .. decided I must run away."

"It was the most sensible thing you could possibly do," the Prince said. "My precious, I will help you in every way I can, but surely you have some relative in England who will look after you, and perhaps one day you will meet an Englishman who will be worthy of you."

"All I know .. is that I will .. never love .. anybody as I .. love you," Katerina said miserably.

The Prince released her hand. "My darling," he said after a moment, "do not make it harder for me than it is already. I am being crucified in a way that I never believed possible." His voice deepened as he went on: "I adore you! I worship you, but I cannot ask you to suffer as my morganatic wife. So we have to say — goodbye."

There was a pain in his voice that made Katerina aware of the agony he was suffering. Without thinking she put up her arms and drew him towards her. "I cannot . . bear you to be . . unhappy," she said. "Let us instead be thankful that we have met each other and known a love which can only have . . come from . . God. If you cannot help me, then I cannot . . help you. You will rule your country wisely, and because you are so . . wonderful your people are . . very lucky."

The Prince made a strange sound and pulled her against him. He held her close in his arms, but he did not kiss her. He only said: "I told you you were perfect — in fact an angel come down from heaven to inspire me. To lose you will be like tearing my heart from my body, and I will never be the same again."

"Perhaps," Katerina whispered, "we could . . write to . . each other?"

The Prince did not answer. Instead, he shut his eyes and just held her against him. She knew how much he was suffering, she could feel his heart beating.

Then, so abruptly that she started, he pushed her aside, got to his feet, and pulled her to hers. "We have all tomorrow," he said, "and then the journey to England. It will be something we will remember all our lives." She knew he was making a tremendous effort not to upset her, or himself.

Then, as he took her through the empty hall and up the stairs, she asked: "What are we doing tomorrow?

Let us make it something very exciting that we will always remember . . like tonight."

"Anything we did together would be exciting," the Prince said, "and for me, very wonderful."

He took her to her bedroom door, but he did not open it. Instead he said: "We have two or three more days together, my lovely one, but be kind to me!"

"Kind?" Katerina questioned.

"I am suffering the agonies of the damned," he said, "but because you are so innocent and so unspoilt you do not understand."

He stood looking at her in the dim light. Then, very gently, he put out his arms and drew her against him. He kissed her forehead, her eyes and her cheeks. Then, without passion, he kissed her lips before he turned and walked away from her without looking back.

As he shut his door behind him Katerina groped for the way into her own bedroom. She could not see because her eyes were filled with tears.

Chapter Six

because Katerina had cried herself to sleep she swore
late. She was then upset of washing time, when she
might have been with the Prince.

When she went downstairs he was waiting for her
and he said, "Now we are going to spend a happy
day together and it will be something we will always
remember."

She smiled at him, finding it hard to do anything
but look at him with eyes of love. She knew that he
was the most handsome, charming and kind man in
the whole world.

When the carriage came round they drove to the
Bois, finally stopping at a small restaurant which
had recently been opened. They had luncheon under
the trees.

They tried to talk. Yet somehow the sentences
would fade away and they would look at each other

Because Katerina had cried herself to sleep she awoke late. She was then upset at wasting time when she might have been with the Prince.

When she went downstairs he was waiting for her and he said: "Now we are going to spend a happy day together and it will be something we will always remember."

She smiled at him, finding it hard to do anything but look at him with eyes of love. She knew that he was the most handsome, charming and kind man in the whole world.

When the carriage came round they drove in the Bois, finally stopping at a small restaurant which had recently been opened. They had luncheon under the trees.

They tried to talk. Yet somehow the sentences would fade away and they would look at each other.

While for the moment they were in heaven, they were both aware that an inexpressible hell was waiting for them when they had to part.

They drove about during the afternoon, then the Prince took her back to the house.

"I have to leave you, my precious, for this evening," he said, "as Prince Charles has arranged a special dinner for me to meet some people he thinks will be of help to Saronia. I know you will understand that I cannot refuse to attend at the last moment."

"No, of course not," Katerina agreed. "That would be discourteous and something you might regret."

"I shall never regret meeting you," the Prince said, "and I want you always to think of me kindly."

"You know I will do that," Katerina said in a low voice.

"I shall know when you are thinking of me," the Prince went on, "and you will know when I am thinking of you. Anyone who has lived in the East is aware of thought transference and that, my precious, is something we will have together."

Katerina remembered her father saying how, in the East, especially in India, the Indian soldiers would say to their officers: "Please, sahib, can I go on leave? My father is dying." When the officer investigated he would find that the man's father lived perhaps three hundred miles away. There could have been no possible communication between the son and his family. Yet he knew that his father was ill.

"I was able to do the same with your mother," Lord Colwin had said to Katerina. "When we were apart I could almost feel as if she was speaking to me, and she would often tell me that I had solved a problem for her because she heard the answer in her heart.

Katerina knew that, in the future, that was what she would do with the Prince. It was poor comfort when they could not be together, but at least she would not lose him completely.

Back at the house he said: "There is one thing I have to do before I leave for dinner."

"What is that?" Katerina asked curiously.

"Take my photographs of you," he said, "wearing the crown jewels."

Because she was not only eager to do what he wanted but also wished to see the jewels again, she went with him into his bedroom.

She saw Prince Michel go to a small jar standing on the mantelpiece and take out a key. He opened what looked like an ordinary cupboard, which inside had been strongly lined.

"Oh, it is a safe!" she exclaimed.

The Prince smiled at her. "Our host keeps his valuables in it when he is here, and I thought it was a wise precaution to put the crown jewels in it." He looked inside as he spoke and went on: "I know I can trust everybody in the house, and Marie and Anton have been here for years and would never allow anyone to steal so much as a piece of paper."

Katerina watched as the Prince brought out the jewel box which he had been carrying when she first met him. He opened it and took out the magnificent crown of emeralds and diamonds. He set it on

Katerina's head. He placed the necklace round her neck and fastened the bracelets on each wrist.

She would have put the ring on herself, but he took it from her. He looked at it for a long moment before he said: "My mother wore this as her engagement ring. If only, my darling, I could give it to you for the same purpose."

There was an agonised note in his voice which made Katerina say quickly: "You said this was to be a happy day."

"Yes, I know," the Prince agreed, "but when I try to be happy I keep thinking of how I shall feel when you are no longer there." He took her hand as he spoke.

Very gently he put the big emerald on the third finger of her left hand. Because she understood what he was feeling, as it was what she felt too, she laid her hand against his shoulder.

Instantly his arms were round her. Then he was kissing her passionately, demandingly, as if he thought the fates which were tearing them apart would separate them at this very moment.

Finally, because time was passing, he posed her in the window.

The sunshine which had not yet faded in the sky enveloped her in a golden haze. She made the diamonds and emeralds sparkle as if they had come alive.

It took him some time to set up his camera. When he had done so he took a large number of photographs, so many that at last Katerina protested: "There will be far too many of me!"

"A hundred would not be too many!" the Prince declared, "and I want them all, every one of them!" Once again she knew he was upset. She did not say any more until he had finished.

Then he put the crown back in its place, kissing her as he did so. When he lifted off the necklace, he kissed the softness of her neck. Because it made her feel as if once again he was lifting her up to the stars she quivered against him.

Finally she whispered: "Darling, you will be . . late for your . . dinner if you do . . not change."

"I want to stay here with you," the Prince said, "kissing you and telling you how much I love you!"

"And I must remind you that your duty to your country comes first!" Katerina answered. She was speaking lightly. At the same time she knew that was undeniably true. If he had not been a Prince and a ruler, they could have been together. She knew they would have been blissfully happy, just as her father and mother had been.

Prince Michel shut the jewel-box away in the safe. He put the key back in the little sèvres ornament which stood on the mantelpiece.

"Now I must ring for Anton," he said, "but I will come and say goodbye to you before I leave."

Katerina left him and went to her own room.

She saw that Marie had left out for her another pretty gown into which to change for dinner. But she would be dining alone.

She felt sure though that Michel would hurry back to her as soon as he possibly could. They could be together again. Therefore as soon as he had gone she would bathe and change. She would be waiting for him downstairs when he came back. The time would soon pass because she had a book to read which she had not yet finished.

A quarter-of-an-hour later Michel knocked on her door. When he came in he was looking, she thought, exceedingly smart. He was not only wearing evening-dress, but also a number of decorations on his coat. A cross suspended on a red ribbon hung from his neck.

"You look very, very impressive!" she exclaimed.

"And you look very, very lovely!" he answered in a deep voice.

He kissed her. Then because they were both aware that he was already a little late, he ran down the stairs. She heard the front door close behind him and the carriage drive away.

It was then Marie came to prepare her bath. By the time Katerina was undressed the water had been brought upstairs. Afterwards she put on the pretty evening gown.

She was ready to go down to the dining room where she was to eat alone.

She hesitated for a moment, looking down at the emerald ring which was lying on her dressing table. She had noticed when she began to undress that Prince Michel had forgotten to put it away with the other jewellery. She had not been aware of it until after he had left for the dinner party.

It was beautiful with the green emerald gleaming like a magic pool in a hidden wood. She thought she would wear it until Prince Michel returned. She put it on her finger again. All the time she was having dinner she was aware of it flashing every time she moved. She felt as she looked into the depths of the emerald that it was telling her something of importance.

She knew it was said that some stones would warn the wearer if they were in danger. She knew too that some changed colour if the wearer was going to die.

Emeralds were her birthstone, and she remembered her mother saying that they meant happiness. But not, Katerina thought, where she was concerned. That was something that no emerald could give her, nor Prince Michel. He would go back to Saronia, and every time he thought of her, she would be thinking of him. But they would be separated and there would be no real happiness for either of them.

When dinner was finished Katerina collected another book from the library, then went upstairs.

Marie had left everything ready for her, including a nightgown which was lying on the bed.

Katerina knew she would not see her again this evening. Both Marie and Anton were growing old and she guessed they would go to bed early.

If Michel wanted anything when he returned Zerge, the new young servant, would get it for him.

Katerina wondered if she should wait for him in the drawing room, but somehow the room was large and empty. She thought it would be more comfortable if she sat on the sofa in her bedroom. If the door was open she would hear him arriving back.

When she was upstairs she suddenly decided that

she would put the emerald ring away in the safe. It would be a waste of time for him to have to unlock it and put the ring with the rest of the jewels. He could be holding her in his arms and kissing her.

She put down her books and walked into his bedroom next door. She pulled off the ring, then took the key from the little sèvres pot and opened the safe.

She needed both her hands to lift out the jewel-box. She opened it and stood looking at the dazzling beauty of the crown. One day, she thought sadly, Michel's wife will wear this as the reigning Princess .. but it will not be me.

It was an agony to think of him having a wife who would give him a son to take his place when he died. Katerina felt the tears come into her eyes. But it was no use crying. Fate had brought them together and Fate was tearing them apart.

She put the emerald ring into its proper place and shut the case. She was just about to lift the box back into the safe when she heard voices. Somebody was coming up the stairs.

Quickly, because she thought it might seem strange for her to have opened the safe, she pushed the door to. Picking up the case she slipped behind the heavy curtains. These were drawn over the closed window. She got behind them and put the jewel case down on the floor under the window.

Then she heard somebody come into the bedroom through the door she had left ajar. "Here we are!" she heard Zerge say in his young, rather high voice, "and what you want is in that cup-board."

Katerina realised to her utter astonishment that he was speaking Russian. She found it hard to believe she was not mistaken, but she could understand what he said. Then a man's deep voice answered in the same language:

"Where's the key?"

"In that ornament on the mantelpiece," Zerge replied. "I saw Monsieur le Prince putting it there when I was watching through the keyhole."

"I'll get it," another voice said, and Katerina knew there were three of them.

She held her breath, thinking it was incredible that the intruders should be there. Also that they were speaking Russian.

There was the sound of movement, then the last speaker said: "This pot's empty!"

Zerge gave a little cry. "Look! The key is in the lock of the safe!"

Katerina knew that all three were now clustered round the safe.

Then the Russian man who had spoken first said abruptly: "The jewel case is not here!"

They must have looked accusingly at Zerge for he said defensively: "I saw him put it there last night."

"Was he carrying it when he went out to dinner tonight?" one of the Russians asked.

"No, no," Zerge replied. "I was in the hall when he left, and there was nothing in his hand."

"Then it must be somewhere in the house," one of the Russians said.

"Wait a minute," said the other. "I have an idea."

"What is it?" Zerge asked.

"Well, it's no use searching the house – it could be absolutely anywhere!" the Russian replied. "The Prince will come back soon and go to bed. Then we'll come and make him tell us where he's hidden the jewels."

"That's a good idea!" the other Russian replied. He must have turned to Zerge as he asked: "You are sure that Mademoiselle does not sleep with him?"

"Quite certain," Zerge answered. "He sleeps alone and she's alone in her room."

"Good!" the Russian said. "And now we'll wait downstairs."

"Are you quite sure it would not be best to search for the jewels?" the other Russian said in a nervous voice. "The German Prince will be very angry and refuse to give us the money he promised if we don't find them."

"The one person who knows where they are is the Prince," his accomplice answered. "Leave this to me – it will not take long to find out what we want to know." He gave an unpleasant laugh as he said: "No jewels are worth too much pain."

"That is true," the other agreed.

"Now we go downstairs very quietly," the Russian who had spoken first admonished, "and while we are waiting the boy can find us something to eat and drink."

"All right," Zerge murmured.

Katerina heard them go from the bedroom. She was, however, sensible enough not to move until she was certain they had disappeared down a secondary staircase which led to the kitchen. She then came from behind the curtain and thought that what she had heard was unbelievable.

The Prince was in danger and she had to save him. Who would have known, who would have guessed, that the new boy, Zerge, would have been half-Russian. He was not, as had been thought, Algerian.

She could understand in a way that Prince Fredrich had, in his opinion, been humiliated and insulted by Prince Michel. Therefore he was determined to take his revenge. Nothing could be more effective than if he managed to steal the crown jewels of Saronia. Prince Michel would have to return to his country and confess that he had lost them.

She tip-toed from her hiding-place, thinking carefully what she should do. First she went to the wardrobe.

She found, as she had hoped, that Prince Michel's evening cloak was still there. Because it was a warm evening he had left for the dinner party without it. It was black and she thought it would cover her white gown and make her inconspicuous.

She knew it was not far to where the fiacres were plying for hire. To engage one was the only way she could reach Michel.

Picking up the case containing the crown jewels,

and concealing it under the cloak, she crept along the passage and down the stairs.

She was sure that at this moment Zerge was preparing food and drink for his two Russian guests in the kitchen. Nevertheless she opened the front door as quietly as she could, trying not to make a sound.

She slipped out into the night. Then she ran rather than walked to where to her relief she saw two fiacres waiting for a fare.

She stepped into the first one almost before the driver knew she was there. He peered in at her and asked: "Where d'you want t'go, Madam?"

She gave him the address of Prince Charles of Monaco's house. She was thankful that she could remember it.

"I am in a great hurry," she added, "so please go as quickly as you can and I will pay you double the fare for doing so."

The driver whipped up his tired horse. They were soon moving at a good pace up the Champs Elysées. It was, however, as fast as Katerina had travelled with the two horses she had driven behind with Prince Michel.

She was praying she would arrive before the dinner was finished. She thought there was no likelihood of Prince Michel leaving yet, but she must make sure of it. At the same time she was praying that her father would help her to save him.

How could she bear the thought of his being tortured by the two Russians? She hated, too, the idea of his losing his precious jewels to the red-faced, boastful German Prince.

"Help me, Papa, help me!" she begged. "I love him and, if I can help him, I will in some measure be paying him back for his great kindness to me."

She felt as if her father was smiling at her and telling her she had done what was right. She was being brave, as brave as he would have been himself in a similar situation.

At last, and in her anxiety it seemed to Katerina a very long time, they reached the house where Prince Charles was entertaining. The horse came to a standstill.

A servant opened the door and came out to see who had arrived. He looked surprised when he saw Katerina, who had not got out of the carriage.

"Good evening, Madame," he said politely, "is there anything I can do for you?"

"Will you please tell His Royal Highness Prince Michel of Saronia that there is someone here to see him on a matter of the utmost importance?" Katerina asked. "I will wait here for him to join me."

She saw the man hesitate. It was as if he thought of protesting against bringing the Prince from the dining room. Then the manner in which Katerina both had spoken and held herself persuaded him that she must be obeyed.

Leaving the front door open he walked across the hall. Katerina was greatly relieved. She had been right in thinking that the men would not yet have left the dining room. They would doubtless be drinking brandy or liqueurs and smoking cigars.

At the same time, she was half-afraid that Michel would think it such a strange request that he would not come.

Then, with a leap of her heart, she saw him walking across the hall towards the front door. The servant was leading the way as he came towards the fiacre.

As he looked inside and saw who was there he exclaimed: 'Katerina! What are you doing here? What has happened?"

Speaking in English so that the servants would not understand, Katerina said in a low voice: "After you had gone, two Russians were let in by the new boy, Zerge! They are being paid by Prince Fredrich to steal your crown jewels!"

Prince Fredrich stared at her as if he could not believe what she was saying.

"They did not find them," Katerina went on, "because I had taken the case from the safe to put the emerald ring back. They are now waiting for your return, and they intend to torture you, Michel, into telling them where the jewels are."

"I find it hard to believe what you are saying!" Michel gasped. "Is it really possible?" Then before Katerina could reply he continued: "Yes, of course it is possible! Prince Fredrich is a bad loser and I think he is utterly and completely despicable!"

"They must .. not hurt .. you!" Katerina said desperately. "Oh, Michel, what will you do?"

The Prince hardly hesitated before he replied:

"Leave this to me, my darling, and get out of the carriage while I send for my own."

"I promised the driver double the fare if he would get me here quickly," Katerina said.

"He shall have more than that for bringing you here safely," Prince Michel replied.

He saw that the jewel case was on the seat beside Katerina and lifted it out. Then he paid the driver. The man's profuse thanks told Katerina that in fact he had been vastly over-paid.

Prince Michel then gave the order for his own carriage to be brought round. Taking Katerina by the arm, he drew her inside the house.

He opened a door in the hall which led into a small room. It was the sort of room that was usually to be found in the front of large town houses while the main reception rooms were at the back or on the first floor.

"Wait here," the Prince said as he put the jewel box down beside her. He then hurried away.

She knew he had gone to make his excuses to Prince Charles. He was back sooner than she expected and with him was a young servant who Katerina thought looked extremely strong.

She saw that he carried a revolver in his hand and that Prince Michel had one too. By this time the carriage which they had used during the day was outside.

The coachman was the same, a different footman was beside him, a big man and broad-shouldered.

The servant handed him another revolver before he

jumped up beside him while Katerina and the Prince stepped inside. The precious jewel case was put on the seat in front of them.

They moved off and the servant who had fetched Prince Michel bowed low as they did so.

The Prince put his arms around her. "My darling, my sweet," he said, "how can you have been so clever as to come and warn me of what has happened? And also, although I can hardly believe it, how is it possible that you speak Russian?"

Katerina gave him a little smile. "It is a long story," she said, "but, please, darling Michel, tell me first that you will not take any risks with these horrible, wicked men! I could not . . bear you to be . . injured."

"Only you could be so brave, so clever, not only to save me, my precious," the Prince said, "but also to save my jewels."

Then as if he could not express what he felt in words, he was kissing her. Kissing her until nothing seemed to matter except that she was close against him. He was taking her heart from her body and making it his.

Chapter Seven

The Prince kissed her until the horses came to a standstill. Then he said: "You are to stay here, my darling, and not move until I come back to you."

"You will be .. careful, very careful ... will you not?" Katerina begged.

"Trust me," the Prince answered.

The man who had come from Prince Charles's house jumped down and opened the door. As he did so Katerina saw that they had stopped not at the front of the house but at the side. She knew there was a narrow passage there leading to the kitchen quarters.

As the Prince got out the footman came down from the box carrying the revolver he had been given. The carriage door was shut and the three men went down the passage.

Katerina could not bear to look any more. Instead

she covered her face with her hands and prayed. She prayed fervently to God and to her father that Michel would be safe.

She knew they would take the Russians by surprise. But that was not to say that they would not defend themselves with knives, or even with pistols.

"Please, God, please . . do not let . . him be . . hurt," she prayed over and over again.

It seemed to her hours before there was any sign or sound of the Prince and the other men. Actually it was less than half a hour. Then at a signal, although she did not hear a sound, the coachman drove the horses up the road until they were in front of the house.

As Katerina held her breath, she saw that the front door was open. Prince Michel was standing there.

She was so relieved that, without waiting for anyone to open the door, she opened it herself and flung herself against him. "You are . . safe! You are . . safe!" she cried. "Is . . everything . . all right?"

"Everything, my darling," he answered.

He held her close to him for a moment. Then he stepped forward to take the crown jewels, which she had forgotten, out of the carriage. As he did so he said to the coachman: "Thank you. I shall not require the horses any more tonight."

As he joined Katerina she could not help asking: "What has . . happened? Where . . are the . . Russians?"

"They are all tied up and will be taken tomorrow to prison. I can assure you, there is no chance of their escaping during the night. They are locked in and the two men who came with me are guarding them."

Katerina gave a deep sigh of relief.

The Prince, having helped her to the sofa in the drawing room, walked to the grog tray in the corner of the room. On it was a bottle of champagne and some other drinks for those who preferred them.

The Prince put a glass of champagne into Katerina's hand before he poured one out for himself. Then he lifted his glass as he said: "We have won, thanks to you, my precious! Prince Fredrich has been beaten once again!"

"It is . . what he . . deserves," Katerina said. "No royal personage should . . behave in that . . abominable way. Those Russians . . might have . . killed you!"

"I think that was unlikely," the Prince said dryly. "At the same time, the kind of tortures they use to make a victim talk are extremely unpleasant, and I am very glad that I did not have to endure them."

"I . . cannot bear . . to think about . . it," Katerina said shuddering.

The Prince sat down beside her. "We will talk of something else," he said, "and the first thing I want to know is how it is possible that you understood what they were saying when they were talking in Russian."

Katerina smiled. "I told you . . it is a long story," she said, "but it just shows that nothing is wasted in life." She knew the Prince was listening intently and she went on: "Many years ago, towards the end of the last century, Papa's great-great-grandfather, when he was a young man, went as a diplomat to Russia." She paused before she continued: "It was in the reign of Catherine the Great, and he was fascinated by what he saw . . and he also . . fell in love."

She glanced at the Prince to see if he was listening and continued: "He fell in love with the Grand Duchess Katerina and, as she loved him in return, they ran away together. It was a terrible journey, for they had to ride for miles before they reached the frontier where they were married."

She gave a little laugh before she said: "Katerina was one of the royal family and the Empress was appalled at an English commoner's presumption in running away with her! They were terrified that they would be captured and perhaps put to death, but eventually they reached England and hid themselves in an obscure little village where they lived very happily."

Katerina drew a deep breath before she said: "When Papa was sent to Russia as Ambassador in 1872, he was naturally worried in case his great-great-grandfather's crime would be held against him. But the Tzar Alexander II took a great liking to Papa and they became good friends." She put out her hand to the Prince and said: "When I was born in St Petersburg, six months after Papa and Mama arrived there, the Tzar insisted on being my godfather and that I should be given the same name as my great-great-grandmother who had run away."

"I can hardly believe this!" the Prince said in a low voice.

"Of course I did not learn Russian then," Katerina said as she smiled at the Prince. "But eight years later we went to stay with Tzar Alexander at the Winter Palace."

Katerina thought for a moment before she continued: "The Royal Family spoke French, but my father always spoke the language of every country to which he was posted. Because he liked me to be multi-lingual, he taught me some Russian on the journey and he and I often talked in Russian long after we had come home. That is the reason why I understood what the Russians were saying who came into your bedroom."

She sighed before she finished: "We stayed with Tzar Alexander for a month, then he was assassinated the following year, so we never went back."

She gave a laugh before she said: "I am very very glad I can speak Russian since it has come in so useful!"

For a moment the Prince did not say anything and she looked at him questioningly. Then he said in a voice that sounded a little strange: "Your ancestor was a Grand Duchess of the Romanov family!"

"Yes," Katerina agreed.

"Her sister," the Prince said slowly as if he was finding it difficult to say the words, "was the Grand Duchess Olga, who married my great-great-grandfather, and it was she who brought with her the Russian crown jewels in which you looked so beautiful."

"Is that .. true?" Katerina exclaimed excitedly.

"It is true, my precious," the Prince said. "What is more, it means that we are related by blood and we can be married as soon as you will allow me to make you my wife."

Because the idea had never crossed her mind, Katerina could only stare at him. Then as he put his arms around her she burst into tears. "I .. I do not b .. believe it!" she sobbed. "I .. I thought that I would have to .. leave you .. and never .. see you again .. oh .. Michel .. Michel .. is it true?"

"It is true, my darling, my precious one," the Prince said. There was a husky note in his voice as if he too was finding it hard not to weep.

Then he was kissing her wildly, passionately. It was as if he felt he had suddenly stepped back from the grave and was alive again.

It was a long time later that they went up to bed.

"Go to sleep," the Prince said, "and you are not to hurry in the morning because I have a great deal to do."

"But .. you will .. be there," Katerina said as they reached her bedroom door. "I am so afraid that this is .. just a dream and in the morning when I wake up you will have .. disappeared."

"I will be there," the Prince promised.

He kissed her again. Then almost as if he was afraid

of his own feelings he took his arms away and walked into his own room.

Katerina undressed slowly, feeling she was in a dream. What had happened could not be real, but a part of her imagination. Then, because she was very tired, she slept.

When Katerina awoke she realised it was late and she rang the bell hastily for Marie.

"Such goings on as I've never heard!" Marie said as she came into the room. "But those wicked men have all been taken away. My poor husband's in a terrible state in case Monsieur le Vicomte blames him for having engaged Zerge."

She gave a snort of anger as she said: "But how could we have known he would be bribed by those criminals?"

"I am sure Monsieur le Vicomte will understand," Katerina said soothingly,

However, all the time she was helping her dress Marie was muttering to herself.

Katerina thought she must talk to Prince Michel about it.

She was downstairs waiting when he came bursting into the drawing room. She thought she had never seen a man looking so happy.

"Where have you been? What is happening?" she asked.

He kissed her very tenderly before he said: "I have a great deal to tell you, my precious, and we both have a great deal to do."

"What is that?" Katerina asked a little nervously.

"First," the Prince explained, "I have been to see your stepmother."

"Oh . . no!" Katerina cried in consternation.

"It was something I had to do," he answered. "When I told her that we were to be married and she recovered from the shock, she became most helpful."

"In . . what way?" Katerina asked suspiciously.

The Prince sat down on the sofa beside Katerina and took her hands in his. "Knowing how you felt," he said quietly, "I made it clear to your stepmother that you do not wish her to come to Saronia, and that, as far as I was concerned, she would not be welcome there."

"Was she . . very angry?" Katerina asked anxiously.

"I made it quite clear that provided she stays away," Michel replied, "she will receive a considerable pension."

Katerina gave a little sigh of relief. "That was very kind of you."

"Then she made a suggestion which I found worth listening to," the Prince went on.

"What was that?" Katerina asked.

"Your stepmother pointed out that if she was not invited to our wedding it would cause a great deal of comment in Paris among her friends, and might injure her reputation." Katerina's lips tightened, but she did not speak. "She also pointed out," the Prince went on, "that it would be difficult, as you are in deep mourning, for us to be married until a year has passed. She therefore suggested that it would be to our advantage, and hers, if we announced that we were married at your father's wish at his death-bed.''

Katerina looked surprised and he continued: "Knowing how much in love we were, he wanted to leave you in my care.''

Katerina was so astonished that she only stared at Prince Michel.

"Because, my beautiful one," he said quietly, "I want you as my wife now, immediately, without any waiting, I agreed to your stepmother's suggestion.''

"But will people . . believe that?''

"They . . will believe it," the Prince replied, "because you and I are already married!''

Katerina's eyes opened very wide. "*Already* . . m . . married?'' she whispered.

"To comply with French law we were married an hour ago in *mairie* and, as is permissible in France, your stepmother stood proxy for you. So that it should be a secret from the newspapers, I was married under one of my other titles. Why should anyone doubt that our marriage took place at your father's bedside?''

The Prince paused for a moment before continuing: "Since the Duc de Soisson would otherwise know it was not true, your stepmother has agreed to say that it happened without her knowledge.''

Katerina was so bewildered that she could not speak and the Prince said gently: "Because I knew you would like it, my darling, I have arranged for us to be married very quietly in a small church just round the corner in an hour's time. The priest is an old man who will not know who I am, but as I have given a generous donation to his church, he could not refuse."

"Oh, Michel, can I .. really be .. married to .. you?" Katerina asked in a broken voice. The tears were back in her eyes and the Prince kissed them away.

"I have never been more happy in my life," he said, "and I want you to be happy too, my precious."

"I am .. I am so .. happy that I am .. sure all this was .. arranged for .. us by .. Papa."

The Prince held her very close against him. Then he said: "While all this has been taking place, your clothes have been packed and will arrive here in a short time. Your stepmother's other suggestion was that I should tell my country when our wedding is announced, that your father particularly asked that you should not wear black for him."

"Papa .. always .. hated black," Katerina murmured.

"And so do I," the Prince agreed. "Fortunately, I hear you have a number of white gowns. However, at my suggestion, your stepmother has gone out to buy you several more from the shops that have your measurements. Some may be here before we leave. The rest will follow after us."

He kissed her forehead before he said: "I told your stepmother to spare no expense in buying you a very lovely gown in which you will be crowned. Although our wedding must be a secret, your Coronation, my darling, will be a great day of joy and celebration. I know that the people of my country will take you to their hearts, as I have taken you to mine."

"I . . am . . going to . . cry again," Katerina said. "I cannot . . help it . . I was so . . apprehensive about . . going to England . . alone, not knowing . . what to do with myself . . not knowing . . where to go . . and having . . no money."

"That is something which need never trouble you again," Prince Michel said. "But you do understand, my darling, we have to be very careful that we carry out your stepmother's plan so that no one will be in the least suspicious."

"What about the servants here?" Katerina asked a little nervously.

"I have thought of that," Prince Michel said. "Of course, they will believe you were already married to me when you stayed here unchaperoned."

"Prince . . Fredrich?" Katerina prompted.

"He found you alone and assumed that you were my mistress. But I shall make it very clear to him that we were married, but it will not be announced until my mother, my Prime Minister, and the Secretary of State are informed I have been secretly married."

Katerina laughed. "Oh, darling, darling Michel," she said. "You think of everything, but Marie has been in such a dither in case the Vicomte is annoyed with them over the Russians."

"I will settle that," Prince Michel said, "by promising not to mention it to the Vicomte. Now go upstairs and make yourself pretty for your marriage."

He looked at her as he spoke and said: "You do

not mind being married in a Catholic church? It is the nearest to the religion we have in Saronia." There was a worried note in his voice as he asked the question.

Katerina once again gave a little laugh. "You will not believe this," she said, "but when I was born in St Petersburg, I was christened in the Tzar's private chapel attached to the Winter Palace. It was of course a Russian Orthodox ceremony. When we returned to England, I was christened again in the village church where Mama and Papa worshipped on Sundays when they were in England."

She saw the Prince give a sigh of relief and she went on: "Papa as he travelled all over the world said that he was prepared to worship in any building that was erected to the glory of God. He was not concerned with the differences of dogma."

"Your father was a very wise man," Prince Michel said approvingly, "and I am only afraid you will find me lacking when you compare me to him."

"I adored Papa," Katerina said, "and I always thought I would never find another man so wonderful. But now I belong to you ... I am part of you .. and I know that our love will never fail either of us, or our .. children." She said the last word a little shyly.

As if the Prince was moved by what she said, he kissed her and there was no more need for words. They belonged to each other completely.

Prince Michel and Katerina drove to the little church and were married very quietly. The old priest made every word of the service seem very sincere and something they would both always remember.

Katerina learned that her husband's names were Alexander Michel. She was married as Esther after her mother, Katerina after her great-great-grandmother and Alice after her father's mother. When she signed the register she found that Prince Michel had been married as Count Dorillo.

As they drove back to the house, the Prince said: "Now, my darling, we are going to spend the first two nights of our honeymoon here, before we set off in style for Saronia."

"What do you mean by – style?" Katerina asked. She was holding his hand tightly, as if she was afraid he might disappear.

"I will let you into a secret," he smiled, "but you are not to tell my relations." Katerina looked up at him and he said: "When I come to Paris I play truant and enjoy myself. I travelled here with two aides-de-camp, a courier, two soldiers to guard me, and my valet."

Katerina gasped. "Wh .. what .. happened to them?"

"I told them all, as I have done before, to take a holiday and enjoy themselves as I intended to enjoy myself by feeling a free man."

Katerina remembered the pretty painted ladies there had been at Prince Charles's dinner-party. She did not have to say anything for the Prince to read her thoughts.

"It will never happen again," he said. "When I come to Paris in the future, my wife will be with me, and if you think I could see any other woman but you, then you are very much mistaken."

"Oh, Michel. I shall be very . . jealous," Katerina murmured.

"Not half as jealous as I shall be," he said. "I only hope I do not have to fight a dozen duels with men like Prince Fredrich, or keep you shut up like an Eastern woman to prevent other men from pursuing you."

Katerina laughed. "You make everything sound so funny," she said. "Oh, Michel, I do love being married to you!"

"And I adore being married to you!" the Prince replied.

They went into luncheon and Marie excelled herself. She was so delighted that they were eating in the house rather than going to a restaurant.

When they had finished the Prince said: "If we are going out this evening, and there is a place to which I particularly want to take you, my lovely one, then I think we should now rest."

"Rest?" Katerina exclaimed in surprise.

When she saw by the expression in his eyes what he meant, she blushed.

"I have had a wife since eleven o'clock this morning," the Prince said, "and now I want to explain to her a great many things she does not know about love."

"Oh . . Michel . ." Katerina began, and was blushing again.

When they went upstairs, she found that her bedroom had been filled with flowers. They scented it with their fragrance.

"I told Marie before we left this morning that we were married," the Prince said, "and that we were keeping it a secret from everybody but her."

"I am sure she was thrilled," Katerina said.

"She said it was the most exciting thing she had ever heard, and at least it will prevent her from going on complaining about the Russians!"

As the Prince was talking he shut the door. Then he said: "When we reach my palace there will be lady's-maids, ladies-in-waiting, and a whole lot of tiresome people fussing about us. But now I have you entirely to myself."

As he was speaking, Katerina could feel him unbuttoning the back of her gown. It fell to the floor and he carried her to the bed.

As she waited for him to join her, Katerina said a prayer to tell her father how happy she was. She told him that everything was like a miracle because it had all turned out so perfectly. How could I have imagined . . how could I have thought for a moment, Papa, she said, that what your great-grandfather did all those years ago could change my life and make me the happiest woman in the whole world?

Michel joined her and as he pulled her into his arms he said: "I know what you are thinking, and I feel the same. We can never be grateful enough, my darling, that we can be together like this, and we must make other people as happy as we are."

"We will . . do that," Katerina said. "Oh . . Michel . . I love you!"

Because his hands were touching her she was quivering against him, and his lips were close to hers. Then as he drew her closer still and kissed her she knew that it was indeed a miracle. She had found the love in which she had always believed.

She and Michel had been made for each other by God. They had found each other in the most unlikely way.

"I love you! I adore you! I worship you!" Michel was saying.

Then, as he lifted her up to the peaks of ecstasy, they entered a heaven that was all their own.

It was all the more precious because, without Fate helping them, they might have lost it.

"We will ... do that," Katerina said. "Oh ... Michel ... I love you?"

Because his hands were touching her, she was quivering against him, and his lips were close to hers. Then as he drew her closer still and kissed her she knew that it was indeed a miracle. She had found the love in which she had always believed.

She and Michel had been made for each other by God. They had found each other in the most unlikely way.

"I love you! I adore you! I worship you!" Michel was saying.

Then, as he lifted her up to the peaks of ecstasy, they entered a heaven that was all their own.

It was all the more precious because, without Fate helping them, they might have lost it.